SPECTACLE

IBSN: 978-0-9850330-1-9

Dedicated to my parents,
who raised a six-foot-two-inch girl
with grace and humor.

1. TALL PRIDE

IT WASN'T THAT Emily Lucas didn't like her jeans; it was that they had shrunk. Or something. This particular pair had been her favorite: a dark blue wash with worn spots on one hip and the opposite knee.

But lately they hadn't been skimming the tops of her feet so much as swinging around her ankles. It was embarrassing, actually, the way they'd gone from Cool to Floods in a matter of a few weeks.

Emily tried not to catch a glimpse of her pant leg as she swung one foot over and off her bike, a heavy '90s Schwinn, brush painted sky blue. She leaned the Schwinn against the porch, trudged inside and dropped her backpack at the base of the stairway.

In the kitchen, she scrounged for a snack that wasn't kale or garbanzo beans, and found a can of diet soda, a jar of creamy Jif (her stepmom's one vice), and a box of crackers.

Plopping down at the kitchen table, she dug in.

"Hey Emily! You're early," Melissa said, coming in and beginning her detailed ritual of brewing green tea. She filled a red kettle with water, measured exactly one teaspoon of dried leaves into a diffuser, and snapped it closed. She tapped it against the counter, then added exactly one more teaspoon of leaves, and snapped it closed again. She retrieved a cup and saucer from the cupboard's top shelf.

Emily, a cracker jammed into the side of her mouth, said, "It was an early release day."

"What for?"

"Teacher meetings or something. I don't know."

October sun streamed through the bank of windows above Melissa's beloved rectangular farmer's sink.

Emily took a swig of soda and said, "I need new jeans."

"Oh? What's wrong with those? And your Luckys?"

"They're shrinking."

"No," Melissa said, sounding mildly devastated. "We're so careful."

Which was true. Emily did her own laundry, but Melissa helped stretch her jeans after every wash, pulling the hems while Emily yanked the waistband, like denim tug-of-war. But it worked. It usually worked, anyway.

"You're growing again," Melissa said.

Emily shook her head, refusing to accept that possibility. "I can't be."

"Let's measure you."

Emily thought Melissa took a weird overinterest in the actual numbers of her height. When someone asked Emily how tall she was, which was often, Melissa would crow, "Five eleven and three-fourths!"

Who cared about the stupid three-fourths?

"C'mon! It'll be … exciting!"

Emily swallowed a large gob of cracker and peanut butter and said, "Unlike you, I don't need specifics, okay? I don't wanna know."

Melissa crossed her arms and leaned against the counter. She nodded. "Denial."

"Fine, whatever," Emily scooped up her snack, went to the family room, and folded herself into the couch.

She clicked on the TV and stared hard at some reality show she didn't care about.

Soon, Melissa joined her and settled herself on the leather chair across from Emily. She flipped her hair, shiny and black. "It's okay to be tall," she said. "You should hold your head up high."

"Tall pride. Got it."

"When I was a kid, I would've killed to be taller."

Right, Emily thought. Tall*er*. Not three-story-house tall. Not oak-tree tall. Not Emily Lucas tall.

She looked at Melissa, whose dainty foot was slung over her knee. She wished Melissa wouldn't try so hard to be her friend. To be all Girl Power. She was ten years younger than Emily's dad and had good music on her iPod, so she thought she and Emily should be besties.

"Can I just eat my snack?" Emily pleaded. "And watch some trashy TV? It's been a crappy day."

Melissa pretended to stare at the show with her for a few minutes, then stood, stretched noisily, and left. She bopped around the house with her earbuds in, straightening, cooking, getting on the computer, and generally being overly cheery.

Just before dinner, Kristen came crashing in, dropping her duffel with a thud on the floor by the front door and disappearing into the bathroom for a shower. She came home just before dinner most days, finally done with whatever practice she was involved in at the time. Volleyball, softball, soccer. It could be any sport. She was good at them all.

Athletic, normal-heighted Kristen.

Emily always wondered how they could be sisters. Really, how?

She went up to her room, kicked the door closed, lay across her bed, and tried to concentrate on algebra. She could smell rice cooking and the fruity scent of Kristen's shampoo.

She heard Kristen's door open and close.

The phone rang, and Emily assumed it was her dad calling to tell Melissa he was going to be late again.

She chewed her pencil, loathing the x's and y's. The numbers that, to her, looked like a jumble of noodles in a bowl. She doodled across the margins of her paper. She thought about calling Trix but decided against it. Trix was probably working at Frederick Hui's, the fabric dyeing plant where she put in 20 hours a week, or wandering Seattle's twilit streets.

Frustrated with math, Emily stood in front of the full-length mirror hanging on the back of her door. There was her long, long body and thin face and big hands.

There was the very-much-not-ideal teenage form. The girl without a petite or sprightly bone anywhere within her skeleton.

Her eyes, thankfully, were bright. Alert. Her henna-brown hair hung in a thick wave past her shoulders. Her lips were a nice shape— kind of full and wide, though she didn't like how they spread like melted butter when she smiled.

Emily could go days sometimes without noticing herself, without catching her reflection in the chrome toaster or a dark store window, without glancing down at her stretched out legs and thinking she was anything other than normal. But then there would come a surprising objective moment, and she could see what others saw: the lanky limbs and how, when she sat with crossed legs, she looked angled and severe. It was a wonder, in a way, that people didn't exclaim more when they saw her, didn't gawk for longer than they did.

She checked out her jeans, at how they stopped too soon now above her feet. She examined her sleeves, which, sure enough, had hiked up an inch or so, showing her bony wrists.

Frustrated, she spun away. How could she be growing again? And how tall was she actually going to get?

2. TRAILER

TRIX OPENED HER window as far as it would go. Sounds from Aurora Avenue filtered in: five lanes of traffic rumbling, the occasional shout, barking dogs. She removed the screen, lit a cigarette and leaned out into the night, a breeze blowing her curly hair off her face.

Trix's mom would flay her if she found her smoking.

Her mother, Fiona Jones, used to smoke herself, but quit when she was diagnosed with early emphysema. Now she filled the nicotine void with food and TV.

Still, Trix was sixteen. She was supposed to try all sorts of things, figure out what and who she wanted to be. Smoking, she had to admit, made her feel kind of badass. It gave her something to do and look forward to.

She thought about the guy her mom was on a date with. Rodney. He had an octopus tattoo on his left bicep. "Look!" her mom had squealed when he came to pick her up, "He can make it swim!"

Sure enough, with a little flexing, the tentacled legs rippled. Trix had smirked and looked away. She couldn't bear the thought of her mom with that guy, laughing at his jokes and swooning over his stupid octopus. But her mom had made it clear a couple years back that Trix had no say in the matter. Fiona'd go out with whomever she wanted, and no amount of protesting or sulking on Trix's part was going to change that.

Fine, Trix thought now, *you go out with who you want to, and I'll go out with who I want to.*

The person Trix really wanted to date was Ryan McElvoy, a cute, quirky, and egregiously decent guy she'd crushed on since middle school. She'd liked him since seventh grade, when she understood nothing about boys except maybe who was nice and who wasn't. And, though Trix probably didn't seem the type to go for a sweet guy, she couldn't help herself. She was drawn to the way he held doors open for people and looked everyone, even adults, in the eye when he talked to them.

Whenever she saw him at school her heart pumped hard and stupid words came out of her mouth.

Sometimes she let herself believe that he could like her back, even though she knew it was extremely unlikely. He was from a normal family that skied and cooked with cilantro and picked up litter on Earth Day.

There was no way he'd give the time of day to a girl who lived in a trailer park on Aurora.

A metallic guitar riff signaled that she'd gotten a text on her crappy old cell phone. It was the flip kind no one had anymore.

Emily: *Bord. What r u up 2?*

Trix texted, *Just hangng*, and noticed her fingernails needed attention. Her purple polish was chipping and her cuticles looked shredded. As soon as she finished her cigarette, she'd fix them.

Wnt 2 come ovr?

Trix shook her head at the phone. As a matter of fact, she didn't. As big and nice as Emily's house was, Trix hated being in it. Emily's stepmother Melissa kept the place perfect—nothing askew, smelling of clean laundry, the kitchen stocked with exotic spices and expensive cutlery. And every time Trix set foot in the McMansion she felt dirty and even more disheveled than usual. She was afraid to sit on the white microfiber sofa or leave lipstick prints on the Crate and Barrel glassware.

U come here.

She knew Emily felt weird at Trix's, too. Trix didn't exactly live in a palace. The rooms were narrow and cluttered. The "front yard" was a makeshift patio lined with fake grass and a short wire fence. And city noise filtered in all day and all night. It was pathetic. Trix couldn't wait to get out on her own. The second she turned 18 she was going to put down a deposit on an apartment or rent a room in a decent neighborhood. She was tired of recognizing prostitutes and living next to Butch's Gun Shop.

Emily texted back that she needed jeans, and did Trix want to hop the bus with her to Northgate before it closed?

Shopping with Emily was brutal. She had this perfectly proportioned but crazy long body. Occasionally she'd find something she was happy with, but reaching that point took eons. Because not only did whatever pair of pants or top have to fit, but also had to pass Emily's cool barometer. Which meant nothing the least bit interesting. No sparkles, low necklines, or short skirts. Trix itched to dress her friend more flamboyantly but her suggestions of ruching or color never went over well.

We wont make it b4 9.

Trix tapped the last bit of ash from her cigarette, then carried it into the tiny bathroom and flushed it.

She got out a shoebox she kept under her bed. Inside were wadded dollars and coins. She added a few quarters that'd been in her pocket and counted the entire stash. A hundred and thirty-two dollars plus some change. She still needed another $196 to buy the sewing machine she had her eye on, a used model at Quality Sewing and Vacuum Center.

To reach her goal, she'd need to stop buying cigarettes for a while, force her mom to pay for the groceries herself from her disability check, and maybe pick up a few more shifts at work.

Once she had the Singer, she wouldn't be limited to lurking around the home ec room at school. She'd be able to bring her designs to life, wear them around, show off a little.

She reached for her sketchbook. There'd been a jacket, short leather, but with a crocheted bustier underneath that had been rattling around her brain for the past few days. She spent the rest of the night drawing, tweaking, filling in colors with her pastels.

She had to absorb the time because, though she'd never admit this to anyone, she couldn't go to sleep before her mom came home from one of her dates.

Finally, at one thirty, when Fiona's keys rattled in the doorknob, Trix shoved the sketches under her pillow and closed her eyes. She hoped her mom wouldn't invite Rodney the Octopus Guy in.

3. CRUSH

"HEY, EM!" CALLED Trix, in her tall black boots and short fake-fur lined coat, catching up to Emily outside the massive, multiwinged brick building that was their school. "Was that algebra homework not impossible?"

"It sucked," Emily said. She rose a good seven or eight inches over the top of Trix's head. "I have to finish it first period."

"I'm not gonna bother. Screw it. When am I ever going to need to know that stuff in real life?" Trix was lying. She always finished her homework, almost effortlessly. She'd been gifted with an amazing memory that made it all a breeze for her.

It was overcast, threatening rain. A typical Pacific Northwest fall day.

"Never. If you're going to be a designer for Betsey Johnson," Emily said.

"No," Trix held up one finger. "My own design house. Remember?"

They walked through the mist into the bright school, which echoed with voices and laughter and the sounds of lockers slamming. Even though the school smelled like stale grilled cheese and moldy paper, Trix was actually glad to be there. Home was too fraught right then.

In the hallway, the girls separated.

Emily twisted her locker combination and got the books she needed for English Comp. Just as she was shoving them into her backpack, Ryan McElvoy appeared. "Hey, Lean Bean," he said.

She pulled the zipper on her pack. Ryan came up to her eyebrows. "The name's Emily," she said. She wanted to call him a turnip or potato or some other stubby vegetable. But, in all honesty, he didn't remotely resemble a turnip or a potato. He was more like a yam or an ear of corn. Kind of ropey and strong.

"I know. But I can have my own special nickname for you, right?"

His nose was long, like a carrot, Emily thought.

He took her in from head to toe.

She was glad her jeans were tucked into her boots that day. So he couldn't see their shrinkage. Or Emily's growthage.

"Leave me alone, McElvoy," she said and sighed. She navigated her way around him and headed for English.

"Ryan just accosted me in the hallway again," she murmured to Trix.

Trix blinked up at Emily, stung, though she tried to hide it. She'd never told anyone, not even Emily, how she felt about him.

Her crush had always been very cloak-and-dagger. She couldn't risk the hurt of finding out for sure that she wasn't his type.

And now Ryan was trailing Emily, Trix's best friend, of all people: teasing her, grinning a lot, and watching her as she walked away.

Trix, to cover her extreme annoyance, started singing the k-i-s-s-i-n-g song under her breath.

"Oh stop," Emily said. "It's the opposite."

"No, he's like a little boy chasing you around the playground. He can't get enough."

Mr. Johnson jumped up from his desk then and began acting out two parts of a play neither Emily nor Trix recognized. He whispered and shrieked and tiptoed and vaulted around. And that was why they loved English Comp and Mr. Johnson. He always made it interesting.

"*Rhinoceros!*" he said triumphantly, finishing his first act. "By Eugéne Ionesco. A drama from the genre Theatre of the Absurd. Can anyone tell me about Theatre of the Absurd?"

Mr. Johnson didn't make kids raise their hands, but no one spoke up.

"Similar to vaudeville, mixed with horrific or tragic images," he said. "Characters caught in hopeless situations, dialogue full of clichés, wordplay, and nonsense. Those are just a few definitions of Theater of the Absurd."

Emily whispered to Trix, "Sounds like my life."

Mr. Johnson yanked a screen down over the whiteboard, tapped his laptop to life, and played some video of Charlie Chaplin, who, he explained, was a direct influence on Theater of the Absurd.

He told everyone to read Samuel Beckett's *Waiting for Godot* and to write his or her own Theater of the Absurd play. Two acts. Due the first week of November.

Trix slipped glances at Ryan and saw him staring at the back of Emily's head (not that he could really help but stare at her head, since it stuck out above everyone's). His eyes glittered.

Trix squirmed. The imaginary ants were back. She had to resist the urge to flick them off her arms and swipe them from her legs. She scratched her back through her sweater.

Johnson jumped around like a fool, reciting something, and Trix's thoughts drifted to the Octopus Guy. Her mom had, indeed, invited him in after their date. Trix's bedroom was barely an alcove shielded from the rest of the trailer by thin drywall, and through it she heard noises she'd rather forget.

"Go home," she'd whispered under her covers. But the clink of beer bottles, giggling, and groaning filtered through the skinny walls. It had been at least three thirty before she'd fallen asleep. And now here she was at eight fifteen with a pounding headache, trying to take in her homeroom teacher's lecture and convince herself that Ryan's interest in Emily was fleeting.

Thanks mom, she thought. *Thanks loser Octopus Guy.*

Filing from class, Emily said, "Can I just jot down everything my dad and step-mom say for my Theater of the Absurd play? That'd get me an A for sure."

"Melissa? She's cool." Trix didn't comment on Emily's father. He was decidedly uncool.

Emily shrugged and said, "She has her moments I guess."

"I'd love to live with Melissa. She's young and hip—way more interesting than my old fish of a mom."

Emily's eyes flashed—a searchlight swooping across her irises. "At least your mom is your *real mom*." As faulty as Trix's mother was, Trix knew her. Lived with her for God's sake.

Emily's memories of her own mother were hazy at best. She'd been four when her mother left and her recollections were nothing more than decomposing mental snapshots. Riding in the car together. Picking her a fistful of buttery dandelions. Hearing her argue with Emily's father in the next room.

Daily, Emily wondered about her, about what she looked like now, where she lived, if she had other kids. Emily had fantasies: that her mother was tall and beautiful, residing in a suburb somewhere, baking cookies for neighborhood children and chairing a garden club, that she was a fashion designer in New York dressing celebrities for premieres, or that she had been in a terrible head-on car accident and had forgotten who she was and that she had two daughters named Emily and Kristen.

Emily had no idea of the reality. She had no clue if her mom was a doting family woman or careerist or really a drug addict strung out in some other state. Or if she was even alive.

Trix and Emily walked down the hallway, talking loudly enough to hear themselves over the din of 1,500 other kids. Trix said, "My mother being real makes everything worse. Believe me, you're the lucky one."

"Trix. C'mon," Emily said. She hated comparing hardships, trying to out-tough-luck each other.

"Seriously. If I could trade Fiona in for the Melissa model, I'd do it in a second."

Maybe Trix was trying to make Emily feel better, but her method wasn't working. Hearing anyone complain about her mom irritated Emily to no end. But when Trix, who knew how desperately Emily wished for a mother, went on about it, Emily took it as open hostility. "Can we talk about something else?" Emily pleaded.

"Jesus," Trix said. "You just need to get over it."

It was then that both of them felt the rumble of the tectonic plates on which their friendship was built. The shudder was brief and almost undetectable, like the ripple of seismic activity before an earthquake. But it happened, causing Emily and Trix to traipse shakily off to their individual classes as if their feet moved across tilting rock.

4. EVIL X-RAY MACHINE

THE DOCTOR'S OFFICE was stark. White paper crinkled under Emily every time she moved. In a rack on the wall were magazines, mostly for little kids: *Highlights. My Big Backyard. Cricket.* One *Seventeen.*

This doctor was a pediatric endocrinologist. Emily's dad, who, unlike Melissa, found her staggering growth infinitely disturbing, had suggested the appointment. Melissa set it up and drove Emily downtown.

The doctor talked to Melissa about things like "bone age" and phalanges and cartilage. He was going to send Emily to the lab to have her hand X-rayed. From the X-ray, the doctor would be able to predict, to a certain extent, how tall Emily would grow.

She'd overheard a conversation between her dad and Melissa a couple weeks before, Emily standing at the top of the stairway while her dad said, "She's going to lap me, M. Jesus Christ. My daughter's an amazon." There was silence then. Until he burst forth with, "We know she doesn't have anything wrong with her pituitary gland, from what Dr. Watkins said when she was, I don't know, nine or ten, but my God. What if she's going to hit seven feet or something?"

Ever the optimist, Melissa said, "WNBA?"

Emily pressed her toes into the nap of the Berber carpet. It was like small, fuzzy peas under her big feet.

"Don't joke," he snapped.

"I'm sorry," Melissa said. "I just don't think it's so bad."

"For her it will be. She's not athletic. She's creative." Emily was surprised her father even knew this.

Sitting in a flimsy gown in this pediatric endocrinologist's office was embarrassing. And Emily was scared of what the X-ray would tell them. She thought she'd rather not know where she'd end up. Kind of like she'd rather not have any inkling of the day she'd die.

The doctor left and Emily was allowed to get dressed. Then she and Melissa took their paperwork down two floors and followed the signs to X-Ray.

The hallways were quiet and squeaky. The exact opposite of the dirty, noisy corridors at school.

A youngish guy in his twenties with red hair and freckles across his nose took the papers. He smiled at Emily and winked. He told her to have a seat, that they'd call her name soon.

Slightly buoyed by the positive attention, however brief, she sat next to a fish tank and watched a bottom feeder slide over the glass. His mouth was a perfect black circle, his whiskers wiggling. She wished she'd brought her camera—an old Canon Rebel she'd gotten used off Craigslist. She would've zoomed in on him and taken a photo of that mouth, gaping like a manhole.

She looked away. She picked up a *Ladies' Home Journal* and read a recipe for cornbread. She stared disdainfully at ads for ugly figurines she imagined old ladies in Nebraska ordering.

When her turn came, the freckled guy led her into a dim room full of machines. A quiet hum filled her ears. With another wink, he left.

An Asian woman arrived and introduced herself as Fay. She instructed Emily to rest her hand on a white table. Fay spread out Emily's fingers.

She laid a heavy lead apron over Emily's chest and left the room.

Emily loved the lead apron. She loved it when she got dental X-rays and she loved its comforting heft now. She wished she could wear it around all day, that she could deflect stares and mean comments with the lead apron.

Within moments, the X-ray tech came back in, removed the apron, and told Emily she could go.

Freckles, on the way out, promised the endocrinologist would read the film and call soon.

Swell, she thought. *I can hardly wait.*

"Want to go to Starbucks or something?" Melissa asked, unlocking the car doors with her remote.

Emily said, "How about Café Obscura?" She tried not to frequent Starbucks. She and Trix had decided it was too corporate.

"Obscura it is," said Melissa.

They drove in silence, listening to a woman singing with a deep, smoky voice. "Who is this?" Emily asked, turning it up a little.

"Cat Power. Hot, huh?"

"Don't say 'hot.'"

"Oh, sorry. Wrong word?"

"Wrong word coming from the wrong person."

Melissa could've laughed at that, should've really. Since Emily was half joking. She'd meant to say "old" instead of "wrong." To joke about Melissa's age. But "wrong" had popped out.

Melissa looked sideways at her and shut off the stereo.

"Sorry," Emily said.

Melissa sped through two yellow lights and got on I-5. Once she'd merged into traffic, she said, "You know, I apologize that I'm not her. I deeply apologize. Because I know you want me to be her. But I am me. Your dad loves the me that I am. And I thought you and Kristen did too. But all I've been getting lately is … attitude. And it's making me tired, Em. It's making me really tired."

Emily stared out the window as they crossed the bridge and passed exits for the University District. She could see, in the distance, the stadium, the Safeco building, treetops that were turning yellow and orange.

Though he never showed it, she supposed her dad loved Melissa. She was reliable. She was pretty for a woman in her thirties.

But there was also something sad about her. She tried too hard. She wanted so badly to be part of Kristen's and Emily's lives that she was always throwing herself in front of them.

Emily said, "Can I ask you a question?"

"Sure," Melissa said, her voice flat.

"Why don't you have a job?"

Melissa made a noise that sounded like a spoon stuck in a garbage disposal. "I do! You know that. I'm a data engineer."

"But you're always … around."

Melissa reached over and gave Emily a light chuck on the forehead. "That's because I work from home, you knucklehead. I want to be there for you and Kristen when you come in from school."

The mood had lightened and Emily was relieved. She vowed not to say another inflammatory thing between there and the house.

Emily leaned her head against the cool window and watched trees and cars whip by. She imagined her mother living in this very same city, over in Wedgwood or down in the Central District, nearly missing running into Emily at Whole Foods or Nordstrom. Over and over. Like the movie *Sliding Doors*.

5. Dad? And a Cat

TRIX BREWED A pot of coffee and fried herself an egg in the kitchen, which was so small she could reach the sink, stove, and garbage can without taking a step. She had her earbuds in and listened to The Bad Fathers.

After eating the egg, she grabbed her coat and purse and went into her mom's room, just big enough for a double bed and narrow dresser. She nudged the mattress with her knee.

"I'm going," she said.

Fiona mumbled something, then opened one eye. "Where?"

"I dunno. Wherever dad deigns to take me this time. McDonald's, probably."

Voice still thick with sleep, her mom said, "You tell him he owes me two hundred thirty dollars."

"Yeah, yeah."

Fiona was always claiming that Trix's dad was behind on his child support payments. Trix didn't doubt he was, but she knew her mother would never see a penny of what her dad didn't feel like paying. Fiona violently distrusted the court system and wouldn't take her father anywhere near a judge. Trix's dad was equally adamant about doling out only what he felt Fiona deserved. Which wasn't much.

Before she left, Trix yanked open Fiona's bedroom blinds. "Trixie, Christ!" her mom shouted after her.

She hustled to the front of the trailer court to wait for her dad. From another double-wide, a baby wailed. Trix lit a cigarette and watched Metro buses, cars, and delivery trucks rumble past. She had no way of predicting how her dad would be that day. Or any day. He could be in one of his jovial moods where he played Lynrd Skynrd loud and drove them up to the mountains for a pseudo-hike, which meant finding a flat two-track road and walking along it for a while. Usually they would then stop at a bar on the way home and her dad would claim Trix was his girlfriend so she could drink. Or he could be in a foul place where he barely muttered hello and dropped her off at the mall while he sat in his truck smoking a joint.

Trix never knew.

Her parents had divorced when she was a baby. Her older brother Vox moved down to Tacoma with friends when he was Trix's age and now tended bar and worked sound at concerts. She only saw him on major holidays. If then. She was pretty sure Vox never contacted their dad. The two hadn't gotten along since Vox hit puberty.

A couple guys hooted at her from a passing Honda. She tried not to care that they might be mistaking her for one of the prostitutes, but she wanted to yell after them, *this is a Badgley Mischka jacket!* What hookers wore Badgley Mischka jackets? She'd gotten it at a thrift store, but still.

She heard him before she saw him, some twangy song blasting from the speakers of his pickup. He slammed on his brakes with a spray of gravel, leaned over the seat and pushed the door open.

"Hey babe!"

"Hi Dad." Trix didn't bother to put out her cigarette as she hopped in. She could be tripping on hard drugs and he wouldn't care.

They zoomed south on Aurora, through three yellow lights, toward downtown.

"Where are we going?" Trix asked.

"A buddy of mine needs help moving a couch in Georgetown. You good with that?"

Her dad wore a t-shirt that showed a band of his heavy, white gut. His frizzy salt-and-pepper hair was tied back with a twist tie. Like a garbage bag.

"Would it matter if I wasn't?"

"Not really," he said, guffawing and turning the music down a notch.

She'd given up being annoyed when he dragged her on an errand or off to a car show she didn't give a crap about. She wanted to spend time with her dad, as sporadic and halfhearted as his attempts at father-daughter togetherness were.

They zipped through downtown, past CenturyLink and Safeco stadiums and finally came to Georgetown—a strip of old brick buildings that housed restaurants and shops, but mostly seemed forgotten, tucked between I-5 and Boeing Field.

Her dad's friend, Buck, lived above a bar and you had to take a rickety, outdoor staircase to get up to his apartment.

As soon as they entered the dusty space, sunlight streaming through dirty windows, a cat with a half tail curling itself around Trix's leg, Buck offered them cans of Pabst.

Her dad took one, but what Trix really wanted was more coffee, not to start drinking and dragging so early in the day.

She bent down and picked up the cat. The backs of his ears were flea bitten and he had no collar. She scratched under his chin. He extended his neck and purred uproariously.

"That's David," Buck said. His laugh sounded like Trix's mom's. Heavy with thirty years of smoking.

Trix cooed his name. "David. Sweet little David."

"Want him?"

She did, as a matter of fact. As soon as he offered, her mind sang, "Yes." But she said, "Oh, nah. I don't think I'm around enough to take care of him."

"You'd take better care of him than he's getting here."

"My mom would kill me."

"Take him!" her dad cajoled. "She'll get over it."

Trix found herself actually considering stealing David home. "Don't I need, like, a litter box and food?" And a flea comb.

Buck tossed her half a bag of Friskies and said, "He shits outside."

And just like that she had acquired a pet. She hung out with David on the curb while her dad and Buck moved the sofa into the back of the truck. Then, all smashed together in the cab with David crawling around their heads and feet, they drove the couch to Beacon Hill and unloaded it into a small white house surrounded by a chain link fence.

Buck and her dad shook hands.

"Can we get a coffee on the way home?" Trix asked.

"What, you want to stop at Starbucks or something?"

"No, I don't do Starbucks. Anything else. Even 7-Eleven would be fine. Just, you know, I need a caffeine fix."

"I thought we'd go back to Nine Pound Hammer." Another Georgetown bar.

For once it bugged her that her dad didn't even remotely observe the legal drinking age. Wasn't a parent supposed to be on top of that? "I'm 16," she said. "Besides. We can't just leave David in the truck for that long."

"He'll be fine."

"Maybe you should just take us home."

Her dad shrugged. "You're the boss."

"I'm not the boss!" she snapped. "I'm the kid."

Except that she didn't feel like a kid anymore. She felt like she had to parent herself, like her mom and dad were the stupid teenagers, too self-involved to pay attention to her.

She talked her dad into stopping at a vet's office on 45th Street, where she waited a half hour trying to hold a dirty, squirmy cat. She left with pills to kill fleas, several vaccinations, and $120 less. Luckily, Frederick Hui was paying her later that week.

She'd gotten a cardboard carrier from the vet, and when her dad dropped her off, she lugged David into the trailer.

Fiona stood in the bathroom doorway doing one of her breathing treatments, which involved a boxy, white machine, a long tube, and a mouthpiece. When she saw David wriggle out of his box and begin prowling around sniffing things, she flapped her hands and pulled the tube from her mouth. "What is that?"

"A cat I just adopted," Trix said, squatting on the thin carpet and trying to coax David to her.

"Oh, a cat you just adopted? Do I get any say in the matter?"

Trix shrugged. "I think he needed somewhere to go."

"Did you even remember that I'm allergic to cats? And I already have enough problems with my lungs as it is."

"You are? Allergic?"

"Yes, Trixie! I always have been." Fiona jammed the mouthpiece back into place and shook her head. She gazed into the mirror and, with her free hand, poked at her sandy brown curls.

Trix decided to wait and see if her mom showed any signs of allergy before getting worked up about possibly having to get rid of David. On the ride home, she'd started liking the idea of a pet, a built-in friend. And then there was all the money she'd spent on him, money that could've gone in her sewing machine fund.

Plus, she figured her mom owed her. She was kind of subpar, as far as parents went. She'd never been one to chaperone school field trips, cook well-balanced meals, get Trix a puppy, or even a goldfish, or supervise her much. The least Fiona could do was let Trix have this one furry thing that already seemed to love her.

6. EXCESSIVE INCHES

EMILY POURED NONFAT milk in a fern pattern across the top of a customer's latté. She'd gotten really good at it the last few months, working at Shutter Joe, half coffee shop, half camera store. Her boss was a flamboyantly gay guy named Thomas, whom Emily loved.

"You're looking glum, girlfriend," he said, once the customer had departed with her coffee.

Thomas wore skinny jeans, a white belt and a tight rugby shirt that totally worked on him. His hair was gelled into small meringue-like peaks, and black liner etched his eyes.

She sighed.

"Wanna talk?"

"It's just, all this," she said, gesturing to her long frame as if she were a prize on *The Price Is Right*.

"All that bodacious girl goodness," he said, resupplying the bakery case with molasses cookies.

Scoffing, Emily said, "Please."

"I'm serious, Em. You got it goin' on. Curves in all the right places. Those crazy long legs. You must have to fight off the boys. Wish I could say the same."

Emily laughed. "Well, it seems I'm still growing."

"You'll be like Brigitte Nielson."

She winced. "Can we say Gabby Reece?"

"Or, you know, yourself, only amplified."

"I'm not an amplified type of person."

A spiral staircase rose above them. It led to a small sitting loft where people often went with laptops or schoolbooks. She stared at the metalwork along the railing.

"Just own it, girl."

Talking to Thomas always made her feel better. Even if there was no way to prevent her growth spurt, at least she had him, who would accept her no matter how tall she got.

She went back to grinding beans, which she'd been doing before the last wave of customers came in.

He stepped up to her, shoved a hand in her back pocket and pinched. Over the grinder, he said, "You know the freakier you get, the more I'll love you."

WHEN EMILY CAME home, Melissa was waiting.

She ushered Emily into the family room, handed her a can of Hansen's raspberry soda and a piece of string cheese.

"What am I? Five?" Emily asked.

"Of course not," Melissa said, and ruffled her dark bob nervously. "I just thought you'd want a snack. You know, like you always do."

"I'm a growing girl."

"Yeah." Melissa paced the room now, back and forth between the microfiber ivory sofa and flat panel TV. "That's what I wanted to talk to you about."

Emily looked at her. She tucked her feet under her butt and sat up straighter. "What?"

"Dr. Haskins called. You know, the pediatric—"

"Endocrinologist," they both said together.

Melissa said, "Right. He read your X-rays and he thinks … he thinks you're still, well, shooting up."

"Awesome," Emily said flatly.

"In fact, his prediction is—,"

"Wait!" Emily yelped. She vaulted to the window. Behind their house was a deep ravine, green with trees and moss and shrubs. When she and Kristen were younger, they loved to explore down there, loved to pretend they were slashing their way through a jungle, watching for snakes and wildcats in the branches.

"Don't tell me."

She heard Melissa inhale. "It's up to you."

Emily wondered why Melissa wasn't beaming, wasn't filled with glee to know that she was still sprouting like an overfertilized sunflower. Dread filled her stomach like wadded up newspaper. The news must be bad. Really bad.

In that moment, she decided. She had to hear the truth. "Okay. What? Tell me fast."

"Six two to six three," Melissa said.

Emily squeezed her eyes shut. Two to three more inches. She was going to grow *two to three more inches.* She would tower over everyone except the tallest of the tall. She'd never have a boyfriend. Girls would be too squeamish to hang out with her. "I'm sure you're happy about that," she said.

"No," Melissa shook her head. "I mean, I think it's kind of neat, yeah. But I know it's really hard on you."

The furnace clicked on, but goose bumps rose up and down Emily's arms anyway.

"Hey," Kristen said.

Emily looked up and noticed her sister standing in the doorway between the kitchen and family room. She rubbed an apple on the hem of her softball jersey.

"You okay?" Kristen asked.

Emily shrugged.

Melissa patted Emily's shoulder and left.

Emily heard her pick up the phone and make a call, speaking in low tones, probably to Emily's dad.

Kristen flopped onto the couch. "You should totally join the track team this year. You'd kick ass on the high jump."

Emily bit her lips, forcing herself not to cry.

"Seriously. You have tons of poise."

"Poise doesn't equal athletic ability," Emily snapped more forcefully than she meant to. Kristen was only trying to be nice. But Emily didn't have it in her to be nice back. Not right then.

She collapsed next to Kristen.

Kristen lowered her voice and said, "How's Melissa acting? Is she bugging the crap out of you?"

Numbly, Emily said, "She's being okay. She actually seems sympathetic. Which just shows you how horrific it is."

Kristen clicked on the remote and said, "Watch TV with me. It'll help you forget."

So they sat through dating reality shows, an hour of dysfunctional crazies living together, and contests where pretty but strange-looking girls competed for a modeling contract.

During the last genre, Kristen raised her eyebrows. "There's always that," she said.

"Right."

"No, really. You're good looking enough to do that. You're way better than those weirdos. That one with red hair? Her eyes are like two feet apart."

Kristen and Emily dug in and criticized every girl on screen, commenting on the chins or brows or shrill voices. It wasn't nice, of course. It was awful and mean and petty. But it made her feel a little better.

Their dad came home around eight. He popped open a bottle of beer, changed into khaki shorts, and stood at the counter eating low-fat tortilla chips that Melissa cheerfully supplied.

Emily stayed in the family room, her eyes trained on the TV. She didn't want to talk to her father about The News. He would treat it as if it were just another hurdle to overcome. *Everyone has issues*, he would say. While inside Emily would know he was mortified.

He came to the doorway and said, "Em."

She looked up at him sheepishly. Kristen had stiffened.

He hesitated for a minute before he said, "So, another couple, three inches, huh?"

"That's what the doctors think," Emily said.

She searched for the tiniest hint of concern etched around his eyes, but she couldn't see any. Bob Lucas was an okay-looking guy, she guessed. For a forty-two-year-old. He'd lost a lot of hair, but what he did have was shaved close to his head. He was trim. He wore silver-rimmed glasses and had perfect teeth.

"Character builder!" he bellowed.

He crunched a handful of chips. He was a fast chewer. Which fit his personality. Always thinking, angling, hurrying.

"Sure, Dad." Emily wished she could disappear into the couch cushions.

"Thatta girl," he nodded and took a swig of beer. His BlackBerry trilled. He answered it and, talking loudly enough for half the neighborhood to hear, went back into the kitchen.

"Thatta girl?" she whispered to herself. Her dad just wanted to acknowledge the news and move on. Do what he thought was his fatherly duty. He didn't care how Emily felt or what she might fear.

Emily, Melissa, and Kristen sat down to a meal of smothered pork chops and mashed potatoes, which were two of Emily's favorites, but a huge departure for Melissa, who usually served things like quinoa with organic chicken breasts and yams seasoned with lime juice. Her dad had moved his call into his office, but they could still hear his voice pulsating through the walls.

Emily politely ate a few bites, but wasn't hungry.

Melissa sipped from her glass of iced tea, eyeing her as she gulped. "It's okay. You want to go?"

Emily nodded and, with tears in her eyes, left the table.

7. INTO THE NIGHT

LYING ACROSS THE twin bed in Trix's tiny room, Emily scrolled through her friend's iPod, listening to a few seconds of a song, commenting on it, and moving to another.

"Anger," she said, staring at the water-stained ceiling. "That's all I'm getting from this. Anger." Emily was into indie pop stuff, a little electronica, and some jazz. She hated a lot of Trix's hard-core rock.

"What's wrong with a little anger?" Trix asked. "We're teenagers, we're supposed to be angry. Rage cleanses the soul."

David was curled up on Trix's pillow, twitching in his sleep.

"No, it doesn't," Emily said. "It just riles up the soul. It feeds on itself."

Traffic whizzed by on 99, practically shaking the walls.

Trix grabbed the iPod from Emily. "What about this one?" she said, choosing a rap that was more catchy than demeaning.

"Eh, not bad," Emily said.

"Oh, you. With all your trip blip clip hop whatever."

In the kitchen, Trix's mom microwaved popcorn, and its aroma filled the trailer, obliterating the nighttime city smells wafting in the window. Trix hoisted herself off the floor, left for several seconds, then came back with two cans of Diet Rite and a plastic bowl filled with popcorn. "Wish these were hard lemonade," she said, referring to the sodas, "but this'll have to do."

They ate and drank for a few minutes, crunching and slurping quietly.

Trix asked, "Should we go out somewhere?" She was restless, feeling too confined by the trailer walls.

"Like … ?" Emily thought of Vera Project for an all ages show, or Dick's for burgers, but neither of those places inspired her enough to stop flipping through tracks.

"I'm not going to Vera," Trix said, reading Emily's mind. "Ben's working there this weekend."

Honestly, Emily wanted to go out, too, to see and blend, to the extent she could, before being just one of the crowd became a complete joke.

Trix said, "I could go for a coffee."

"You could always go for a coffee."

"Yeah, well, it's something."

So Trix and Emily grabbed their bags, said goodbye to Trix's mom—who ate popcorn with one hand and held the remote with the other while watching a medical drama on TV—and went out into the night.

8. PARTY

"WELL, WELL, WELL," Trix said from the table where she and Emily sat at a coffee shop on 80th. "Look what the mangy old cat dragged in."

Emily turned and saw Ryan McElvoy. He caught her eye and flashed a mischievous smile.

She gripped her white, porcelain mug hard, burning her fingertips. Kind of liking the sting.

"McElvoy!" Trix called. "Why the hell aren't you somewhere with beer and hot chicks? This place is for losers."

"God, Trix," Emily hissed.

Ryan sauntered over, shoving his wallet into his back pocket. He rested his hands on the back of Emily's chair. "You two don't look like losers to me."

"We are," Trix said, smiling a little too brightly. "The biggest." She felt the ants again, in her hair this time, skittering across her scalp. Maybe she'd caught David's fleas.

Ryan stood back, "I guess that makes me the biggest lameass, then."

"You said it, not me."

Emily was struck mute, unable to find a way in to Trix and Ryan's exchange.

"I bet money you're just passing through. On your way to a party. Am I right?" Trix said, her heart jackhammering.

"Over in Wallingford. Jason Bleak's."

"I knew it!"

Emily hated how overly boisterous Trix was around guys. How she turned into a ridiculously animated version of herself. Emily had to admit, though, that her approach seemed to work. Guys responded. They liked the attention, she guessed.

"You coming?" Ryan said.

Trix gazed into her coffee and all but stuck out her lower lip. "Not invited." A party was just what she was in the mood for.

"Who cares," Ryan said, hearing his name and starting for his beverage, which sat waiting on the counter. "You know Jason. He'll be totally slizzard. He won't even know. He won't care. I guarantee it."

Trix tossed off a playful little shrug.

Ryan glanced at Emily and said, "You're coming, right, Lean Bean?"

"Wallingford?"

"Yep. Behind QFC on 48th."

"Maybe."

Emily's coyness drove Trix crazy. It wasn't like she had Evites flying into her mailbox. What could it hurt to check out one little party?

"Cool." He waved and dashed out to a waiting Hyundai just before it squealed away from the coffee shop.

"Whaddya think?" Trix asked. "Want to take the 358 to Wallingford? Crash the shindig?"

Emily shook her head. There were too many variables that could turn Trix's plan into disaster.

1. It could be a small get-together, just a few guys with a case of beer.
2. Parents could show up.
3. Trix might end up drunk, which would force Emily to get her home and clean her up, something she did not at all have the energy for.

"We're not invited, remember?"

"It was probably an open call. Anyone can show," Trix said.

Emily was torn between going along and coming off as a buzzkill.

Then she remembered her doctor's appointment. Six foot three. Would she even have the guts to enter rooms full of snarky guys and sneering girls when she was that much taller? Would she become a teenage shut-in, homeschooling online and socializing only through Facebook?

"Okay, for a little while," she muttered.

THE PARTY AT Jason Bleak's, as it turned out, was big. There were at least 100 kids. Some Emily and Trix recognized from school, but many faces were new. Rap thumped through invisible speakers.

A group of guys stood to the left of the door, near a potted ficus, slamming beer from plastic cups.

"Hey, Big Bird's here!" someone shouted.

Emily froze.

Trix prodded. "It's okay," she said. "Ignore them."

The swirling crowd pushed the girls forward. But Emily's face was hot, her feet heavy.

Trix felt bad for her friend when it came to making public appearances. People could be so rude. But she didn't want to turn around and go home, either.

A girl wearing a black hooded sweatshirt and a blue streak through her bangs instructed Trix and Emily to pay ten dollars, handed them cups, and pushed them toward a silver keg.

They found a spot in the dining room and sipped their beer. "Not bad," Trix said. She could easily chug six of them. Fast. The fizz felt great sliding down her throat. Soon the invincible warmth that came when she drank would envelope her, and all would be right with the world.

Emily thought the beer tasted like dirty socks filled with old coffee grounds. Dutifully, though, she sipped. It wasn't that she was dead set against drinking; she just wasn't wild about the flavor of beer and didn't have any desire to end up sick and spazzy the next day like she'd seen Trix.

"Any sign of Ryan yet?" Trix asked.

"Ryan? Oh, uh, nope. No sign." Emily tried to pretend she didn't care. But she couldn't help scanning over everyone's heads, looking for him.

"Maybe in the basement?"

"Look," Emily said. "It doesn't matter. We didn't come here for him. We came here to get out of our coffee house rut."

Trix said, "Right. But it'd be nice to bump into him, yes?" She was hoping to bump into him herself. Preferably without Emily.

"Whatever." Emily was grumpy and already sick of the spastic throng of giggling girls and sloppy boys. The music was giving her a headache and she felt horrendously tall.

"Drink more," Trix said. "It'll help."

So they stood around and slurped beer. Trix gestured a lot with her hands and laughed crazily if Emily made an even slightly amusing remark.

After a while, Trix half turned and involved some guy, who went to Seattle Prep, in their discussion of, of all things, jigsaw puzzles. Trix thought he was cute. Just the right mix of rebellious nonchalance and intensity.

"Yeah, dude," he said, "I once put together this mammoth 5,000-piecer. It was of Snoqualmie Falls."

"By yourself?" Trix asked doubtfully.

The guy, blond, hazel-eyed, nodded and said, "Every last piece."

"Wow, impressive," Trix said.

Emily couldn't tell if she was being serious or sarcastic but decided to give her the benefit of the doubt. Maybe she liked this guy.

Soon, Trix was talking more to him than to Emily. Oddly, though, Emily was okay with it. The beer was working its magic, making her feel less raw, more open, like she'd accept anything that came her way: another Bud Light, a chat with whoever staggered by. Even a tall joke wouldn't hurt as much as it usually did.

Other kids eddied around them, eating chips and laughing, but mostly drinking. Jessie Turner and Zeke Masey stood together in a corner kissing. His hand gripped her thigh, just below the curve of her butt and both of Jessie's arms were wrapped around his shoulders. They were into it. Nuzzling and kneading with their fingers. Even from there Emily saw the flick of their tongues. She couldn't look away.

"They need to get a room, eh?" said a male voice.

Emily turned and found she had to tilt her head up. He stood a good four inches taller than she did, had bushy black hair, a wide, horsey jaw and eyes so sunken she couldn't tell if they were blue, brown, or some color in between.

"Yeah," she said. She whirled the dregs of her beer around her cup, as if she were tasting wine and holding a fragile stemmed glass.

"Talk about PDA," he said.

"It's a little over the top."

He shook his head and took a long swallow of beer. "How do you know Bleak?"

"Oh, Jason? I just … he goes to my school. We were invited by one of his friends."

"That's okay. I'm sure most of the people here don't even know who lives in the house. I'm Sam, by the way."

"Emily."

"It's nice to talk to someone who's not, you know, a midget."

"Yeah," she said.

The music thumped so loudly she could hardly hear him. She had to lean in when he spoke and his breath was warm across her ear.

"Bleak and I have known each other since we were this big." He lowered his hand to toddler height. "Well, maybe I was up here." He raised his palm. "My sister's about five eleven, six foot. Same as you?"

She nodded, a little self-conscious of Sam's and her combined stature. She imagined people looking over and thinking, *Of course* those two *are talking. Of course.* She asked, "What does she think of it?"

"Oh, she digs it! She plays basketball, volleyball, goes out for track. The whole deal. So it's a huge advantage for her."

"Like my sister," she mumbled. Why didn't she care more about sports? It would make her life so much easier if she were coordinated, fast, aggressive.

"So," he said. "Cannon High, then. You love it?"

Emily shrugged, "It's … just … classrooms and lockers and a bunch of kids. Some mean, some nice."

"None in between?"

"Probably," she said. "Me, I guess." She looked over at Trix, hoping she was done with the blond/hazel guy. But, not only was Trix not done, she'd slipped further into the shadows and was gazing up at him adoringly, nodding at everything he said.

"That your friend?" Sam asked.

She nodded.

"Looks like she's gonna hook up."

Emily swallowed hard. She glimpsed Jessie and Zeke again, still groping in the corner. A thought flashed through her mind. Hadn't Ryan McElvoy dated Jessie for a while?

The site of her with Zeke now made Emily queasy. Was this what always happened at these parties? Was the main goal to get drunk and stagger around looking for something to make out with?

She regretted agreeing to leave Trix's house that night, regretted hopping on the 358 and taking it over to Wallingford.

She said to Sam, "I'm sorry, I'm just—"

"Hormonal?" he said and laughed, a machine gun ra-ha-ha that set Emily's teeth on edge.

"I was going to say tired."

"Oh, right." He laughed again.

And a little envious and a little disappointed that you're not someone else. And yes, tired too, she thought.

"Hey, need another beer?" he asked.

"I think I've had my fill." She turned and took a step away from him. "It was nice to meet you though."

"Wait," he sputtered, still having to shout over the music. "Mind if I call you some time? It's not often I meet girls I can see eye to eye with."

She was both flattered (it wasn't every day, or EVER, that a guy wanted her phone number) and bummed (that the guy who wanted her phone number was condescending and kind of ugly).

She considered giving him a wrong number, a trick Trix sometimes pulled. Or she could take the high road and say *No thank you,* or maybe lie about some imaginary boyfriend, but in the end, she didn't know how to reject him to his face and said, "Sure, I guess."

"Well, don't act so excited," he said. But he didn't seem flustered. He whipped out his cell phone. "Okay," he said. "What is it?"

As Emily rattled off the numbers, he punched them in.

She said, "Well, I think I'll head out. Past my bedtime." She turned to Trix and hissed into her ear, "I'm ready whenever you are."

Trix poked her in the ribs and said, "Silly girl."

"Seriously," Emily said. "This isn't really my scene."

Trix looked at her then, "Your *scene*? What are you? From the '70s?"

"I just want to go, okay?"

Scowling, Trix said, "Well, you might want to go, but I don't." She wanted Ryan to see her with this guy and think, *Who's Trix Jones talking to? Maybe it should be me.*

"Okay, I'll get back myself." Emily spun and tried to push her way toward the door. Wherever the door was.

She'd made it through two rooms when she stopped in a promising-looking hallway. Dead in front of Ryan.

He had no beer. Both hands, in fact, were buried in his pockets. "Hey, Lean Bean," he said, a small smile playing on his lips. "You made it."

The party was still rollicking around her. She knew that, but the noise and laughter faded away, like school-play scenery that had been pushed off stage to make room for the next act. The act in which Emily realized she liked Ryan McElvoy. A lot.

"Yeah," she said. "But we're ... Trix is ... I'm on my way out."

"No fun to be had here?" he said.

Against her will, she felt herself smile. "I've had my fun. And now I'm finished."

His eyes were incredibly blue. She thought of the book they'd read in English last year, *The Bluest Eye.* The Bluest Eyes.

"How are you getting home?" he asked.

"Bus."

"Alone?"

"That's the plan."

He said, "I'll walk with you to the stop."

"You don't have to. Really. Who's gonna mess with *me*?"

He laughed and jerked his head toward the door. "You might be surprised. Let's go."

Fog had descended, casting Wallingford in a gray shroud, streaked by the glow of yellow streetlights.

The footfalls of Emily's All Stars and of his leather shoes echoed as they walked.

He said, "You don't strike me as a partier."

"I don't?" She didn't know if she should feel offended or complimented. But just the fact that he'd formed an opinion about her partying likelihood sent a chill up her spine.

He shook his head. "You don't seem like you need to drink to … have a good time … or to be, you know, cool with yourself."

It was Emily's turn to say, "You might be surprised." Being okay with herself was something that seemed entirely out of reach right then.

The bus stop was three blocks away and they went most of the distance talking about stupid stuff: classes and homework and the drunken idiots back at the party.

Just as they came to the covered bench, which had been tagged in red spray paint, she asked, "What about you? Are you the type to get smashed often?" She honestly didn't know. He didn't seem to have a reputation either way.

He shrugged. "Have I ever? Yes. Do I make a habit of it? No." Moving closer to the yellow sign marked 358, he said, "Thanks for not being stupid."

"What do you mean?"

"Thanks for letting me walk you. Bad things can happen to girls by themselves at night."

Emily laughed. *You're not stupid* might've passed as flattery in third grade, but now it was kind of lame. Still, Ryan was cute and it had been nice of him to watch out for her. "I guess."

"Don't let anyone tell you otherwise." He did this thing where he stuck out his jaw and rubbed his stubbly chin.

It occurred to her that he had to shave. Guys her age fell into two camps: those who shaved and those few stragglers who didn't need to yet. That he fell into the first group thrilled Emily.

He stopped on the curb, underneath the bus sign.

"You don't have to wait," she said.

He looked at her then and their eyes locked. Her browns and his gleaming blues. "Now why would I walk you all the way here and not wait with you?"

"I don't know, I just thought—"

"Well stop thinking," he said. He took a step closer. She could smell his breath, some miasma of mint and *boy*.

She swallowed hard.

Just then the bus's brakes let loose with a hydraulic squeal.

Damn.

She glanced at the driver, an androgynous character in the standard issue navy uniform, then back at Ryan. "Well … thanks," she said.

Quietly (regretfully?) he lowered his lids and said, "No worries."

She fished her metro pass from her bag and got on. As she moved down the aisle, the bus jerking forward, she saw Ryan turn and walk back toward Jason Bleak's house, hands still in his pockets and head down.

Had he been about to kiss her? Had she been about to kiss him? She hoped beyond hope they'd find their way to a moment like that again. Because she wanted to see it through.

9. TRYST

TRIX WAS ON her fourth beer and Devlin was being so nice. He fetched her a new drink whenever she wanted one, talked to only her in their little corner, and rubbed her back with his knuckles. She felt taken care of. Warm. Wanted.

The rest of the party was a blur around them. All color and noise, nothing that mattered except that its existence allowed this pocket in which Trix and Devlin could chat and steal the occasional kiss.

"You want to go somewhere quieter, so we can talk better?" he asked.

Trix loved that idea. Her voice was hoarse from shouting over the music and she was tired of getting body slammed by drunken kids. "Let's go," she yelled.

Devlin took her hand and they weaved through the crowd to a small, dark room with a washer and dryer, ironing board, and furnace. Well, she thought, it's not the most comfy place in the house, but at least it's private.

He led her to a pile of blankets and spread them out into a little nest. Then he wrapped his arm around her and they listened to the muffled music. She thought she could stay there forever, his hand draped over her shoulder, the side of her body smashed up along the side of his, both with fresh beers.

"I really like you," he said.

"So I gathered," Trix quipped. Wait. No. She was going to drop the sarcastic shtick and try to really talk to this guy. "I mean, thanks," she said. She couldn't bring herself to say, *I really like you, too*, but she did run her hand along his thigh. These moments with other guys helped her forget about everything else. And Ryan? He was a distant speck right then.

Devlin leaned forward and kissed her. A real kiss.

When he pulled back, he said, "I have something to ask you."

"Yeah? What?" Trix just wanted to keep kissing him.

"Will you be my girlfriend?" He gazed at her, his head cocked.

And it was that, the tilt of his head, just a degree or two too far, that caused something in Trix's brain to flicker: he's full of it. He just wants to get in my pants.

But she was enjoying the closeness and the making out and the clean smell of detergent. "Are you serious?" she asked.

"Of course. Dead serious."

"We just met."

"I know, but we have a connection. We're, like, completely hooking up on this whole other level." He used his hands to demonstrate a higher plane. "I mean, most kids our age are way down here, but we're linking way up here."

Despite her doubts, she wanted to believe him. She wanted to believe him more than she'd ever wanted anything.

He continued, "I mean, I want your body. But I love what's up here, too." He began massaging her temples. And Trix's brain melted until she was nothing but a shell descending on Devlin, pulling his mouth toward hers.

A FEW VOICES still whispered and cackled. A cold draft swept across the laundry room floor and wreathed Trix's body.

Devlin snored on the pile of blankets.

She sat next to him, naked and hugging her knees. She wondered if she should sneak out and let him sleep. But, no. She wanted Devlin to acknowledge what had happened. Leaving would make it too easy for him.

She nudged his ribs.

Mid-snore, he jerked upright. "Man," he said. He stretched. He scratched his scalp. "What time is it?"

Checking her crappy cell phone, Trix said, "Two-oh-seven."

"Wow, I gotta go."

That wasn't the response she'd been hoping for. She wanted more kissing, more hugging, more of, "I want your body. But I love what's up here, too".

She'd known, though, that after the fact, she wouldn't get those words. She'd seen the pickup line as if it had been a prompt he read off a cue card, and she'd wanted him anyway.

He stood and held out a hand to help Trix up. This cheered her briefly. Until, still holding her hand, he began to shake it as if they'd just concluded a business meeting. "Hey, thanks," he said.

She bit her lip and looked toward the dryer with its gaping circular mouth. "Yeah, sure."

"It was fun. I mean it. Serious fun."

Nothing about being his girlfriend. Of course.

She was never convinced that guys who made promises about future relationships meant them, but she liked to think, at least for a couple hours, that she was lovable.

Big deal, she told herself. It was just sex. Just body parts. Apparently this was how the world worked, and she might as well get used to it.

Devlin gave her a last wave and left her there, surrounded by bottles of Tide and boxes of Bounce. Scorned by the snug accouterments of a functioning family home.

She'd wait a few minutes before she followed him out.

As she stood there in the dark, her brain reeled. Devlin had been her seventh guy. Or was he her eighth? God. And Emily was still a virgin. How had her best friend managed that?

And how did Trix and Emily happen to be best friends? It seemed that they were diverging down different paths—Trix careening into adulthood and Emily on this lateral, moving sidewalk. But then, Trix really shouldn't criticize Emily's failure to evolve. Ryan McElvoy was paying more attention to Emily than to her, wasn't he?

The ants came back, scampering all over her inner thighs and down her calves. Trix thought she might go insane trying to scratch them all off.

10. HOSTILITY

THE NEXT MORNING Emily's dad woke her by rapping her doorframe and belting, "Up!" He did not believe in lazy mornings.

She stood and pulled a sweatshirt over the Top Pot Doughnut t-shirt she slept in. She couldn't wait until she was in college and could sleep as late as she wanted on weekends.

As she was brushing her teeth in the bathroom that connected her room and Kristen's, her cell phone buzzed.

A text from Trix.

WHR DID U GO LST NGHT?

Emily typed in: *HOME! Duh.*

She washed her face and went downstairs. She was the only one in the house who drank caffeinated coffee, so she made herself a cup with the French press.

"Want some steel cut oatmeal?" Melissa asked from where she stood at the stove. "I put flax seeds in. Add a little kefir and mmm."

"Is that supposed to tempt me?" Emily sat at the table with her creamy coffee. "How about some Bisquick waffles? A few slices of bacon?"

"Oh, Emily," Melissa said. "That stuff's horrible for you. A growing girl needs her steel cut and her kefir."

"I don't want to grow anymore, thanks anyway."

"Right." Melissa caught her lip between her front teeth. She used a wooden spoon to scrape the sides of a pot.

From outside came the lawn mower's drone. Emily peeked out the window and saw her dad pushing it angrily back and forth across their wide yard.

Part of what made Emily's extreme height seem so unfair was that no one else in her family was especially tall. Her dad had stopped just short of five nine. And Kristen was average. So Emily had to skulk around being a cypress tree, all alone. The closest any other girl in school came was Jessie Turner, who was somewhere around five ten, with milky blond hair and amazing bone structure. And an apparent ability to draw guys like flies to honey.

Emily's mom lingered in the kitchen like an apparition. Emily would've liked a mom to talk to, one who would wake her up sweetly in the morning with a gentle brushing aside of her curtains, and who would understand the challenges that came from being a tall girl.

The story of how her mother had left was family lore now, The Unraveling of Marilyn Wozniak Lucas. She took money from the bank account, painted stars all over the station wagon, and stocked up on this Guatemalan tea sold at her favorite food co-op. (They were able to piece this together after a neighbor saw her buying copious amounts of the peculiar purple boxes.) Still, Bob Lucas didn't catch on.

On a misty Monday morning, she drove away while Emily's dad was at work and Emily and Kristen, four and five, were with a babysitter.

Emily could remember only dark snippets of what happened next. Her father arriving home in the middle of the afternoon and making lots of phone calls. A police officer showing up, looking so big and official standing in their doorway, scribbling in his notepad. Kristen holding her hand tightly as they sat on the swings in the backyard, waiting to find out what had happened to their mom.

The answer they needed never came. Confusing days passed during which Emily and Kristen were shuffled to different neighbors. Casseroles and quiches filled the refrigerator. Kristen's first grade teacher even took them both out for ice cream.

Now, the pining for her real mom made Emily hate her pseudo-replacement a little.

She lashed out at Melissa, "Don't you ever, you know, indulge in a Pop-Tart? Why are you such a health food Nazi all the time? It's tiresome."

Melissa didn't seem fazed. "I'm just trying to take care of this family. Lord knows you need taking care of."

Emily leveled her gaze at Melissa and said, "I'm sure we'd do just fine."

Melissa's head jerked up, as if she'd just been pricked with a pin, voodoo style.

The turning of the wheels in Melissa's brain was almost visible. *Ouch. Pretend it's okay. Emily's just a kid. Cut her slack. Cut her slack. Cut her slack.*

Melissa continued stirring her steel cut oats.

Emily said. "I'm being a brat. You can say it."

Melissa stirred harder. "You know," she said. "I do my best around here. I understand the fragile relationship between a stepmom and stepdaughter. I just don't get why you're always on me." Emily thought she heard Melissa's voice catch.

Then, as if she were thinking aloud, "Kristen seems okay with me."

Emily could smell the fresh mowed grass through an open window. "I don't get it either."

Kristen swooped in then and grabbed an orange from a wooden bowl on the table. She wore a cute, splashy running skirt and a tank top and looked athletically adorable. Tanned, blond, big-boned in an attractive, Scandinavian way.

"Can I have some of that oatmeal?" she asked Melissa.

"Yes," Melissa said, a victorious lilt to her voice. "Yes, you certainly may. It's just about ready." She looked pointedly at Emily and raised her brows.

Emily smirked and said, "I'd still rather have Pop-Tarts."

The landline rang and Kristen, being closest, answered. She held out the phone. "It's Trix. For you."

Emily realized she'd left her cell upstairs and that Trix had probably been trying to call her on it. She rolled her eyes.

Trix said, "Hey. Who was that tall drink of water you were talking to last night?"

Emily had been so annoyed at Trix for slobbering all over the blond guy, and so distracted by walking to the bus stop with Ryan, she'd forgotten all about Sam. "Oh," she said. "Just some childhood friend of Jason Bleak."

"Did he get your digits?"

In that moment, Emily decided Sam was okay, if only because his interest allowed her to participate in a conversation where her best friend asked if a boy had "gotten her digits." Wasn't that what high school girls were supposed to talk about? Supposed to focus on? Not on inches and stretching jeans and runaway moms.

Suddenly, Emily felt a surge of euphoria. She was, however briefly, a normal teenager. And she had to laugh at Trix—crazy, maddening, Trix. "Yeah, I guess he did."

Emily wouldn't tell her about Ryan. She didn't want it out there to be picked apart and banged up and analyzed. Not yet anyway. "Promise you'll never make me go to another one of those things?"

"Another party? Oh, you'll go to more parties. There are lots of parties in our future."

"How'd it go with Mr. Blondie? You seemed pretty into him."

Trix's voice twisted a little when she said, "Yeah. He's okay."

"You sound weird. Are you all right?"

"Why wouldn't I be?" Trix sighed. "Except I need to talk. Get some stuff out. Are you free today?"

"Yeah, I just … I wanted to take pictures."

"Meet me at Green Lake," Trix said. "You can snap away while we walk."

Emily agreed, though a little reluctantly. She'd been looking forward to some alone time with her camera. Time to think about last night, to deconstruct her conversation with Ryan, to relive each step between Jason Bleak's house and the bus stop. But Trix didn't sound right.

They planned to meet at one.

Emily hung up and, while Kristen ate her steel cut oatmeal with flax seeds and kefir, poured herself another cup of coffee.

11 . REGRET

GREEN LAKE WAS crowded, as it always was on sunny weekends. Parents pushed babies in strollers along the concrete path that fully encircled the small body of water. Inline skaters zoomed and weaved, and bicyclists called out, "Coming up on your left!"

Trix and Emily held coffees as they walked, and every so often, Emily would pull out her camera, squat, and snap a picture of a goose, a kid on a tricycle, or a fisherman.

Trix was quiet, wobbling a little in her three-inch wedges. She said, "I mean, it's not that big a deal, right? Everyone does it."

A cool breeze ruffled their hair.

"Right," Trix continued. "Well, not you. Not *everyone*. But most of us."

Emily knew Trix was being a jerk because she'd done something last night that shamed her. But her words flooded Emily with a feeling she hated: of being the only one. Of being left out of something big.

"You put out, didn't you? You did something with that guy you shouldn't have. And you're trying to make me feel like the pariah. I can see right through you, Trix."

Trix scowled. She hadn't said it to hurt Emily. More to justify herself. "I didn't say you were a pariah." Then, yanked by a grabby jealousy that her friend got to be the "good" one, the one with the fancy house and cute, wholesome boy paying attention to her, she added, "Though if the sneaker fits ... "

Emily stopped on the path and people streamed around them. Bicyclists glared. If there was one thing she most hated about Trix, it was this: how she tried to deflect her insecurities onto other people, usually Emily.

Trix added, "If a hottie like that was hitting on you, you'd be all over it, too."

A cloud drifted across the sun and Emily felt cold. "I didn't think he was a hottie. He had hard eyes."

"Hard eyes? What the hell does that mean?"

As angry as Emily was, she sensed that her friend needed her right then. She looped one of her arms through Trix's and propelled them forward. Trix resisted at first, not wanting to be cajoled out of her anger. She staggered slightly as she pulled back. But then she gave in and walked.

Emily said, "It means his eyes weren't soulful. I didn't see much in them, Trix."

"It was dark," Trix argued.

"Not that dark."

"You were drunk."

"One beer?"

"He wasn't so bad," Trix said, but her fight was obviously fading. They went several hundred feet in silence. Then, quietly, she said, "He got up and left right after ... we did it."

"Where did you ... do it?" Emily asked, not at all sure she wanted to know.

A seaplane rumbled above, heading for Lake Union to the south.

Trix admitted, "At Jason's. In a laundry room."

"Oh, Trix."

Trix started sniffling. "I know. I know, okay? So don't say it."

Right then, Trix didn't seem irreverent or daring or admirable at all. She just seemed sad. A girl ditched a few minutes after having sex with a boy she barely knew. Emily muttered, "What a skank."

"That's probably what he's saying about me right now."

Emily had the urge to offer advice like, *what goes around comes around*. But, frankly, she didn't have enough experience to say much of anything. She'd never had sex, or even come close. How did she know what it'd be like in Trix's shoes?

Instead, Emily asked, "Did you ... did he use a ... ?"

"Yeah," Trix shook her head to banish the memory. "Yeah. He had a condom in his back pocket. Thank God."

"Would you have, if he hadn't had one?"

Trix wanted to yell, "No! Of course not!" But the fact was, she didn't know. She got so caught up in moments. Especially if she was feeling good and having fun and basking in someone's flattery.

They came upon a family walking four abreast across the trail. Trix and Emily stepped up on the grass to skirt around them.

"I want you to be my girlfriend. I like more than your body, I like your mind." Trix mimicked Devlin, then made a gagging sound. "Please."

"Maybe he'll call," Emily suggested.

"No. I could tell. He was done. He got what he came to the party for."

Emily felt bad for Trix. Trix had been in this position more than once, and each time she moped for days afterward, feeling slutty and dirty and used. And each time, Emily told herself she'd never, ever get herself in the same situation.

She did something unforgivable then. She took off her lens cap, crouched and snapped a rapid succession of photos. She had to. Trix's expression was so wan. So vividly conflicted and sad.

And Trix responded exactly how Emily expected. She kicked out her foot hard, just missing the camera by a slim few inches.

12. THE RUNAWAY'S DAUGHTER

THAT NIGHT EMILY dreamed her mom was standing in a bright, wheaty field, wearing a sundress—the kind a little girl might. Her face was generic—all the features in their right places, without forming a recognizable person. Exactly how it was in Emily's memories.

Her mother didn't see her. She just crouched and picked wildflowers—Queen Anne's lace and black-eyed Susans—while humming a lullaby.

Emily called to her, waved at her. But her mother didn't notice.

As Emily ran toward her, her mother vanished and reappeared further out in the field. A mirage she couldn't reach.

When Emily woke, she was moaning quietly, buried under her covers.

How could she be motherless? How could her mom have painted stars on their car and left her two daughters and husband? And where was she now? Was she even alive?

With daylight, the intense pain of the dream cleared a little, but didn't disappear entirely.

Emily thought of Trix and her sporadic dad who showed up once every few months to take her for a ride in his truck or to dinner at Red Robin. But at least he came around. At least she knew what he looked like and could ask him questions and see the hazel flecks in his eyes.

Getting out of bed, Emily tiptoed into Kristen's room.

Her sister slept on her stomach with one arm thrown over the side of the bed, fingers grazing the carpet. Her blond hair was pulled into a ponytail and she breathed quietly.

Sitting cross-legged on the floor, Emily watched Kristen. Her room was, not surprisingly, different from Emily's. Messier, but, at the same time, sparse. Clothes, jerseys, and sneakers lay over her bed's footboard, and across the floor.

Kristen's dresser top was mostly bare, sporting just a softball trophy looped with rubber bracelets. A wilted gerbera daisy hung over the edge of a murky glass of water. A physics textbook laid open.

Rain pattered on the roof. Emily was actually glad for it. Glad for the excuse to stay in. She knew that soon all their days would be overcast and wet, but, after a sunny Pacific Northwest summer, she was ready. The weather matched her mood.

"Krissy," she stage whispered. "Krissy."

Kristen stirred, turning her head toward the wall.

Emily heard the front door open and close and knew it was Melissa, heading out for her morning run.

She hissed her sister's name again.

This time, Kristen, in a gravelly voice, responded, "What?"

"I had a dream about Mom."

Kristen lifted her head and looked at Emily. Less irritated and more sympathetic, she said, "Really? What was she doing?"

"She was in a field, picking flowers. And humming. I couldn't get to her, no matter how fast I ran." It sounded dumb, voicing it. But Emily knew Kristen would understand better than anyone.

Kristen said, "I've had that dream. Except she was at a gas station, filling her tank and buying Doritos and I was locked in the bathroom. The door had a window. I could see her and I was pounding to get out. But she never heard."

Emily shivered. She liked her own version of the dream better. "God," she said.

"I know."

Kristen's room smelled like dirty laundry.

"Do you think about her much?" Emily asked. "I mean when you're awake."

Kristen considered this for a minute then flopped back onto her pillow and gazed at the ceiling. "Sometimes. I try not to."

"I have been lately. More than usual."

"I wonder why."

A bird yodeled from outside Kristen's window. The house hummed—appliances and digital clocks and heaters.

Kristen said, "Did you know that Mom's dad was, like, six eight?"

"I knew he was tallish, but ... really?" Emily said. "I wish I remembered him." Both of her mom's parents had died too young. In their fifties, she thought.

They had no photos of them, not even a dusty Polaroid.

The few pictures they had of their mom were taken in the early nineties. The jeans were high waisted and tapered at the ankles. The hair was still big, left over from the previous decade. And their mom's face looked squinched and forlorn.

In one shot, she rested her chin on the top of Kristen's head and looked into the camera, her eyes swimming in tears.

In another, she sat at a picnic table with their dad, his arm draped over her thigh as he studied her profile. But she stared at something outside the frame of the picture. Maybe, in her mind, she was already on the road.

13. HASSLED

TRIX WIPED SWEAT from her forehead and took off the ink-covered smock she wore for her job at the textile-dyeing plant, Frederick Hui. She stuffed the smock into her locker, bought a vending machine soda and sat on the hard wooden bench that served as break room seating. She usually put in about 20 hours a week. Which was the only way she got any spending money for clothes, music, and other necessities. She also had to buy several bags of groceries a month to supplement the meager junk her mom stocked the cupboards with (namely, lots of microwave popcorn). What was left over went into her sewing machine fund.

Luckily, schoolwork came easily for Trix. She had a memory like a Venus flytrap. Except that instead of grabbing and quickly digesting bugs she swallowed facts whole and never let them go. Otherwise she wouldn't have been able to pull off her job plus any sort of social life.

Still, even with her nifty brain, Frederick Hui was a lot of work, and Trix, in that moment, felt overwhelmed. She was tired. Sometimes it seemed she'd lived a long life already, full of regrets and angst and hurt feelings.

She took a long drag from her soda. She had ten minutes before she had to get back to her shift.

Originally, she'd taken the job because she wanted to do something related to fashion. And at sixteen during a recession, dyeing fabric was the closest she could get. Someday, she told herself, she'd work with the same fabrics she dyed. She'd drape them over models' bodies, gathering here, stitching there. Just thinking about the possibility excited her.

As she imagined her future, Aaron, a guy in his twenties who always had a toothpick in his mouth, came into the break room. He didn't bother to remove his smock. Instead he sprawled out on another hard bench and groaned.

Over the top of her soda can, Trix watched him.

"How old are you?" he asked without looking at her.

"Thirty."

He laughed. "Seriously."

She told him her real age.

"Get out," he said. "You're still young. Don't get sucked into this place. It's a velvet coffin. A dang velvet coffin. They make it seem all nice and cushy and then they trap you with the money and bonuses and you can't never get out."

Trix thought "nice and cushy" was pushing it. Just look at the barren break room. The money was pretty good though. She made more than most of her friends who worked at cafés or shops.

"I'm okay," she said.

He poked his ever-present toothpick around his molars. "Are you?"

She shrugged. She wasn't about to tell Aaron how thrashed she felt. How she wanted to take her next paycheck and get a nice hotel room with thick walls and a squishy bed and sleep for 24 hours. Maybe she'd take David with her, feed him straight tuna out of a silver dish.

She thought of Emily and how she got to sleep in a place like that every night. She had a big, mod bedroom done in plum and lime, lush carpeting, and a bathroom with a Jacuzzi. You wouldn't be able to feel an earthquake in that place. Much less a car rumbling past.

Aaron raised himself up and asked for a sip of her soda.

"Get your own," she said. The last thing she wanted was his cooties all over her can.

"But I only want one drink. And you have a whole 16 ounces. I can see the condensation there on the side. It's making me all thirsty."

"Do you want to borrow a buck?" she said, getting irritated.

"No, not really," he came to her bench and sat down next to her. His eyes had gone glassy.

A bad feeling rose up in Trix. She tried to scooch back on the bench, but found she was at the very end.

Aaron leaned in closer. "Just a little sip," he said and licked his lips. He reached out, but instead of taking the soda, he rubbed Trix's denim-clad thigh and moved his hand between her legs. She went to jerk away, but he held her down, leg pinned to the bench.

"I'm so bored here," he said. "Just give me a little sip. Just a little sugar to help get me through."

She held her soda can over his crotch and dumped out the contents.

"What the hell?" he cried, jumping up and swiping at his pants. "Now I look like I pissed myself!"

"You're lucky I don't report you for sexual harassment, you asshat!" Her heart thumped hard, but she did her best to look cool. She couldn't let him see that he'd freaked her out.

"Christ, don't," he said to her, his eyes now clear and desperate. "I need this job."

"Get out of here," she said in a low steady voice. "If you ever come near me again or I hear of you pulling this crap on anyone else, I'll pour a lot more than soda on your dick. And I'll make it my personal mission to get you canned."

He emitted an animal-like cry of frustration. "I didn't mean nothin'. God! What a bitch!" he yelled. But he left.

Trix got up slowly. She kicked the empty can so it rang against the metal lockers. Why did this stuff happen to her? Nothing so seedy would ever happen to Emily. Did Trix put out a vibe that said, *White trash! Hurt me. I'm used to it?*

Grinding her teeth, she went into the bathroom, peed, and splashed her face with steaming hot water. She put her smock on and went out onto the floor again, the smell of chemicals and sound of whirring, clacking machinery greeting her.

She wanted a new life. She was sick of this one. All she needed was a plan, some way to transport herself out of the doldrums she was stuck in and to an existence with a little more sparkle.

14. If I Could Chat with Anyone, it'd be You

ONLINE SHOPPING FOR jeans didn't really work. Not in Emily's opinion anyway. She needed to try the jeans on. Look at her butt in a three-way mirror. See if they clung to her just enough, but not too much.

That morning she was at one of the household's two computers (there was Melissa's laptop, which she had taken over, and a full Mac upstairs in a small loft just off the stairway landing). She browsed sites she knew sold extra long jeans and put the clothes on virtual models, but, when it came down to it, she couldn't submit the order.

She clicked over to her Facebook page. She didn't log on everyday. The updates were mundane, the cliquishness like an extension of school, right there in the kitchen.

But Facebook was necessary. If not for Facebook, she'd be completely clueless at school, listening to other kids talk about links or videos she didn't understand because she hadn't checked her news feed.

This time she saw she had two friend requests waiting.

The first was from a girl, Julia Noma, who'd gone to Whitman Junior High with Emily, but then had moved to Wyoming. *Accept.*

The second ... and her heart started thumping faster ... was from Ryan.

She squeezed her eyes closed and told herself, *Big deal. Big deal. So he wants to be your Facebook friend. He's probably friends with everybody.*

She went to his profile page. Three hundred and eighty-two friends. Of course.

Favorite movies: *Napoleon Dynamite, The Bourne Trilogy, School of Rock, O Brother, Where Art Thou?.*

Okay, so he had decent taste in flicks.

Favorite music: (*Please no rap, no rap, no rap*, she thought.) Cake. White Stripes. Beck. Coldplay. Death Cab for Cutie.

Favorite books: *The Curious Incident of the Dog in the Night-Time*, Anything Nick Hornby, *Choke* by Chuck Palahniuk, *A Heartbreaking Work of Staggering Genius* by Dave Eggers.

She sat back in her chair. So much of what he liked was what she liked. God.

She read his favorite quote: "Happiness does not depend on outward things, but on the way we see them." –Leo Tolstoy.

Emily quickly looked to see if Trix was online. She wasn't.

She wrote her an email: *Ryan just friended me on FB!!*

Then she deleted it. She didn't want Trix to know that Ryan's friend request was important to her. She didn't want to give Trix reasons for not-so-covert glances at school or the possible slippage of Trix's tongue.

She was just about to log out of Facebook when the chat window opened. And there was Ryan's photo—a black and white shot of him holding skis—next to his name.

She read: *Emily, my new friend. Thank you.*

She typed back: *How could I not?*

Ryan: *You could've refused.*

Emily: *Why would I?*

Ryan: *You could've sent me a personal message that said, 'I'm not friending you, lameass.'*

Emily: *If u were, in fact, a lameass I might have.*

Ryan: *So your opinion of me is one notch above lameass?*

Emily: *Maybe a notch.*

Ryan: *Relief.*

There was a long pause, where Emily reread their exchange.

Emily: *What are u up to today?*

Ryan: *I just helped my dad fix the garage door. Now I'm drinking lemonade and looking for new music on iTunes.*

Emily: *Bon Iver?*

Ryan: *I'll check it out. What about u? U finish that homework for Johnson's class?*

The dark thought that maybe Ryan was trolling for homework help struck her and she recoiled from the screen. People more or less knew what kind of grades everyone else earned. So, he probably had a good idea that Emily was up there near the top of the heap.

She didn't want that to be true, that he was using her. She decided to give him the benefit of the doubt.

Emily: *Theater of the Absurd assignment? No. But it shouldn't take too long. U?*

Ryan: *Did it Friday afternoon. H8 having that stuff hanging over my head.*

Emily: *I know what you mean. Yet, I let it hang. Am lazy.*

Ryan: *I find that hard to believe.*

Emily: *It's true.*

Ryan: *Okay, gotta split. A bunch of us r going to Myrtle Edwards Park. You know, before the weather turns to complete crap.*

Emily stifled her disappointment. She pounded out: *Which should be any day now.*

Ryan: *Any minute.*

Emily: *Have fun!*

Ryan: *U too. Doing whatever you're gonna do this afternoon.*

Simultaneously, they wrote "Bye." And she logged off and jumped away from the computer, as if spending more time on it would tarnish the chat she'd just had with Ryan.

Melissa strode into the kitchen, still in her running spandex. She mopped sweat from her forehead and said, "You look spooked."

"I just," Emily started, faltered, then tried again. "I just don't know what to do about jeans."

Melissa took a long drink from her metal water bottle. "How about if you and I go shopping?"

Shopping with Melissa wasn't on Emily's list of desired Saturday activities. "Where?" she asked, doubtfully.

"Pacific Place?"

The risk of running into people she knew at Pacific Place was too high. "Southcenter?" Emily suggested. It was farther away and had more stores.

"Really?" Melissa said. "That's way down there." She took another drink, then said, "Unless—oh. That's your point."

Emily looked up at her guiltily.

Melissa said, "Okay. Southcenter. Just let me shower and grab a bite to eat."

"We could get something down there," Emily suggested.

Shaking her head, Melissa said, "Unless I can get tuna on rice cakes with a kale smoothie chaser, I think I'll eat here."

"Nasty."

"Yeah, yeah," she started upstairs. "Just wait until you're in your late thirties. You'll start doing whatever you can to slow it down."

Emily knew she'd never resort to eating like that. Where was the joy in tuna and kale?

Besides, late thirties? She couldn't even wrap her mind around *mid twenties*. Where would she be then? Grad school? Dating? Would she have a boyfriend, or be left behind while all her friends furiously got married and popped out babies?

"Never!" she called after Melissa. It was going to be Pop-Tarts and peanut butter and jelly the whole way through.

15. HOME ALONE

TRIX FELT LONELIER than ever.

1. Her mom was out with the Octopus guy again.
2. Trix had, of course, no boyfriend to occupy her.
3. And virginal Emily was being all high and mighty, texting that she was going to lay low and have a quiet night at home.

Trix lay on her bed, smoking cigarette after cigarette, too despondent to even get up and turn on the TV.

She needed to diversify. Emily couldn't be her only/best friend. They were growing too far apart.

She thought about how they'd first started hanging out in seventh grade. Emily, tall and rangy, was sitting in the cafeteria eating an apple and reading a book. Trix was new to the school, having just transferred up from Fife.

Three girls, now known as the Farkettes, were across the table from Emily, ganging up, asking if she played basketball or volleyball, and telling her she looked like a walking toothpick.

Trix hated seeing anyone picked on. She was the type to collect strays and try to protect them. She approached the group. Emily looked up at her with hopeful, fearful eyes, unsure if Trix was there to join in the abuse or befriend her.

"What's wrong with being different?" she yelled at April Kinsmith, the trio's clear ringleader. Trix hadn't quite honed her rhetorical skills into the jagged barbs they would become. "You want everyone to look like you three? I can't imagine a more boring world."

Emily had given her a nervous smile. "It's okay," she said.

"No, it's not. These girls need to learn how to treat people. And how looking like a bland middle school clone isn't what anyone should strive for."

"Coming from you," April said, "I'll take that as a compliment."

True, Trix was wearing her faux-snake skin heels, super-flared jeans, and a purple peasant top covered by a velvet shrug. But she loved that outfit. "Get over yourselves," Trix said. Then to Emily, "You ready?"

Emily wrapped her apple core in a napkin, closed her book, and followed Trix out onto the school's lawn. It was spring term and kids were playing hacky sack and lying on the grass soaking in as much sun as possible before clouds rolled in again.

"Um, thanks," Emily said. "I think."

"You think?"

"I was doing okay. But I appreciate your trying to help."

"Doing okay? They were all over you like dogs on a dead squirrel."

"Well, I mean, I was using my obliviousness strategy."

Trix cocked out her undeveloped hip and said, "It wasn't working. They needed verbal bitch slaps."

Emily laughed and Trix did, too.

After that, they began seeking each other out at lunch and soon, outside of school. Over the last few years, their friendship had morphed into what it was now. Trix wondered if it had run its course.

David the cat was curled up on Trix's feet. She sat, grabbed the flea comb off her chipped dresser, and began to rake it across his back. Every time she found a flea, she flicked it into a bowl of soapy dishwater she'd been keeping next to her bed for drowning purposes. She'd discovered an odd satisfaction in hunting down the fleas and killing them.

Her thoughts drifted to Ryan. Quirky, handsome Ryan. While Trix snagged all the skeeves who just wanted to hook up and throw her away like a snotty tissue, Emily got Ryan. Or was on her way to getting him.

David yowled and hissed. Trix realized she'd been pushing down too hard on the comb. She let up and tossed it back onto her dresser.

Why couldn't she just walk away from this and let Emily live a little? Why did Trix have to begrudge her?

Because she'd liked Ryan for so long. And she was insecure. She hated feeling she wasn't worth as much as Emily because Emily's dad had money and she was blooming into this pulled-together, statuesque beauty and a normal guy liked her.

The question was, could Trix stop herself from trying to destroy what her friend had?

16. FIRST DATE

ON MONDAY NIGHT, Sam, the tall guy from the party, called Emily. She answered her cell, already knowing it was a Sam Stone, but pretending she didn't. She let him explain himself, how they'd met.

"Oh, right," she said. "Hi."

"How's your week going?" he asked.

"Well, considering we're only one day in, I'd say fine."

He asked about classes. About what public high school was like, if it was true that CHS had its own bowling alley.

"No," Emily said. "That's a rumor."

"Oh." He sounded disappointed. "I was hoping I could talk you into showing it to me."

Her mind suddenly spun fast. *He was going to ask her out. Of course he was. Why else would he have called?*

Yet, despite her desire for interaction with the opposite sex, she found herself shrinking away from the idea of spending time with him. Alone.

How would she handle this? She could lie and say she had a boyfriend. She could flat out say, "No, thanks." She could pretend to be sick.

Then the question came, "So, think you'd be up for a movie or something Friday?"

Emily thought of Ryan and how she wished he were the one on the other end of the conversation. Ryan McElvoy who was a good couple inches shorter than she was. Right.

"A movie?" she said.

"Yeah. The new James Bond."

"James Bond?"

"I've seen it twice and it's awesome. You game?"

Emily frantically racked her brain for an excuse, but in the end, she squeaked, "Okay." Her first date. At sixteen. And not with someone she would've chosen. But, as Trix would say, *Chalk it up to experience.* God knew Emily needed some.

That week flew by in a blur of homework, strained run-ins with Trix, and a walk through Fremont where Emily took tons of photos and, later, spent hours editing them on the computer.

When Friday night rolled around, she searched hard for something decent to wear. For almost an hour she tried on shirts and shorts and skirts and a pair of khaki pants that had fit the fall before, but now made her look like a geeky ten-year-old boy whose mother forgot to go shopping.

She turned around and around in front of her full-length mirror and swore and threw clothes in a pile next to her closet door.

Finally, she settled on a denim skirt that hit just below midthigh, black tights and her favorite black Banana Republic sweater that was stretched out and faded, but super comfy.

When she trotted downstairs, wearing more eyeliner than usual and some actual lip gloss, her dad saw her and said, "Good God."

Horrified, Emily ducked into the bathroom and slammed the door. She sat on the toilet, head in her hands.

She heard Kristen tell their dad to leave her alone.

After a few quiet minutes, Emily eked the door open, grabbed her backpack, and ran out of the house.

"Be back by eleven!" her dad called from the living room.

At seven o'clock, the streets were already close to dark. The bus, when it came, was lit inside and looked like a traveling airport terminal, full of people reading and waiting, bored stares plastered across their faces.

Normally Emily would read too, would pull out whatever book she was required to make it through for English Comp. But she couldn't focus, so she just gazed out the window.

When she met up with Sam, he gave her a once over and led her into the theater. Emily couldn't help wishing he were Ryan. Ryan, with that introspective something that made her swoon.

During the movie's funny parts (and there were only a few), Sam treated her to his explosive ra-ha-ha-ha laugh that made Emily want to sink down in her seat. Except that there was no legroom. And her knees already jostled his. Which she hoped he didn't take as a sign of interest on her part.

Afterward, they walked to a bar called Dynamite that Sam swore he could get them into. She didn't have the crazy, try-anything rush she sometimes got when she was out with Trix and in a good mood and high on the city and her youth, but she decided she may as well see the night through.

Dynamite looked more like a vintage clothing store than a club. Mannequins stood in the windows wearing gold lamé, tall boots, and feather boas.

Emily and Sam sat on retro acrylic stools and drank a beer at the glass and chrome bar. Sam made a joke and laughed his ra-ha-ha laugh.

And then he did it. His lips pressed against Emily's and they were watery and thick and cool.

His tongue, fat and slimy, pushed past her teeth and wiggled like a thick worm trying to dig a hole.

Her first instinct was to pull away and wipe her mouth, but she forced herself to sit there and take it. To experience it.

Later, on the way home, Emily called Trix who churlishly assured her that if the kiss was that gross, Sam didn't know what he was doing.

Emily noticed that Trix was doing a lot of long inhales and exhales on the phone and guessed what she was up to. "Are you smoking again?" she asked.

Trix had smoked a lot when they were freshmen. But that next summer, after her mother had been diagnosed with early-stage emphysema, Trix had decided cigarettes were beneath her and, to Emily's relief, quit.

"I'm a teenager! I'm just experimenting. Jesus!"

"Well, just … don't. Don't get yourself hooked. You're better than that."

Trix took another long drag and said, "Am I?"

17. MEAN GIRLS

EMILY AND TRIX hated their gym teacher, Ms. Stark.

The woman was teeny. Four foot ten, which, in itself, was fine. But she was also wispy as a dandelion stem, mean, and thought it was her job to make a spectacle of Emily.

During the volleyball unit, for instance, she instructed Emily to demonstrate a serve. A serve that didn't make it to the net the first four times she tried. Finally, on the fifth hit, red and humiliated, Emily knocked the ball over.

Trix had watched, feeling cooler toward Emily than she ever had, and a little smug that Emily was making a fool of herself. She knew it was terrible of her, but couldn't make herself stop smirking.

Ms. Stark, whom Emily and Trix had dubbed Fark because it was fun to derisively roll the word off their tongues, commented on Emily's height constantly, calling her Stretch, Tall Drink, Amazon, and Sasquatch.

Emily couldn't think of anyone who made her more uncomfortable.

Besides maybe the Farkettes: Vanessa Beam, Kennedy Furukawa, and April Kinsmith, a trio of *bi-otch* who lived to fling their bodies around the smelly gym and make life hell for anyone not up to the same tasks.

Emily and Trix sat against the wall in PE that afternoon, actively disregarding a gymnastics unit in which everyone was expected—just because Fark used to be a gymnast herself—to learn cartwheels and handstands and walkovers. Emily couldn't manipulate her body into any such formations.

And Trix didn't care in the least about her PE grade.

"So," she said as casually as she could. "Any more word from Ryan?"

"What do you mean?"

"I mean, are you an item yet? He seemed pretty into you the last time we saw him."

"Oh," Emily said, sensing a bitterness in Trix's manner and making up her mind right then that she wouldn't tell her about their walk to the bus stop or their chat on Facebook. "No."

"Really? I thought you might be going at it already." Trix felt mean, but couldn't stop herself.

"Why would you think that?"

Trix shrugged. "I just imagine at this point you'd take whatever came your way." She hoped this would imply that Ryan was *whatever*, not someone to be coveted.

Emily said, "I can see right through you, Trix. You're deflecting. And I hate it when you get like this."

In front of them, three sets of long, still summer-tanned legs appeared, tapering gracefully into silver and blue Nikes. Trix looked up, already sneering.

"This too much for you girls?" Vanessa asked, her arms crossed. Her cronies, Kennedy and April, stood on either side of her.

"As a matter of fact," Trix said. "It's hella retarded."

Vanessa, Kennedy, and April were favorites of Fark. Once, and Emily was pretty sure this was illegal, Fark had left the three girls in charge of the class while she ran an errand outside the school.

"It's only retarded if you can't do it," April said.

"Why don't you go back to humping the mats?" Trix said, picking at the black polish on her fingernails.

Emily laughed, which she couldn't help, even though she knew her laughter would draw the ire of the three Farkettes.

April turned her attention to Emily and said, "It would be quite a sight to see you flipping around those uneven bars. With your hands and feet hitting the ground every time you went over. Like an ape's."

Trix stood. However she was feeling about Emily, she couldn't abide that kind of abuse.

Emily said, "Trix. Whatever. Don't worry about it." She whispered, "They're losers."

"Oh, we're the losers?" April said. "Ha! Yeah, us. While your best friend here lives in a shack on Aurora."

"It's a traaaaylllloorrrr," Trix said, enunciating each letter. "Not a shack. A trailer. Get your facts straight."

April muttered, "Same thing."

Trix said, "Actually, April, they're very different. While a shack connotes something that is fundamentally run down, a trailer is merely an architectural style. Trailers can be nice. Not that mine is, but still."

Emily grinned, forgiving Trix in that moment for her recent surliness.

Kennedy had remained mute, hanging back the tiniest bit from April and Vanessa. But still, right along with her friends, she looked at Trix and Emily as if they were moldy chunks of Gorgonzola.

"Whatever," April said.

"Go whatever yourself," Trix said. "I'm sick of your fake baked faces."

April scoffed and the three girls pivoted and walked away.

Trix had won the battle of words, of course. She always did. But, really, in the great, ridiculous, popularity skirmish that was high school, she'd lost.

She and Emily both had.

18. CRASH

OUT OF HABIT, Trix and Emily still gravitated toward each other. God knew Trix didn't have many options of who to spend time with and she wasn't good at being alone.

That day, as usual, they went to Fatty's, which was just across 65th, for grilled cheese sandwiches and fries.

The day was overcast, the clouds so low Trix felt like she could reach out and grab handfuls. An ambulance whizzed past, its siren wailing, lights bouncing off windshields and windows.

Inside the tired, little restaurant that was supposed to evoke the '50s, but just came across like a used up movie set, Trix and Emily placed their orders, then found a table.

Emily had finally decided to tell Trix she was thinking of trying to find her mom. She wanted to say it aloud, to make it real. And she thought it might help bridge the chasm that had begun gaping between her and Trix.

Before she could stop herself, Emily blurted it out.

Trix coiled one of her curls around her index finger and let it go, then checked her crappy phone. No calls. She set down the phone and looked right at Emily. Trix didn't know what Emily expected. A round of applause? "Good for you," she managed. Though she felt the ants crawling again. How nice to have a fantasy mom out there that you could just invent to match what you wanted, and then decide, *Oh, I'm going to find her! And everything will be great and we'll live happily ever after.* Emily didn't have to deal with a sketchy father who only showed his face once a month and never, ever acted like a real dad. No, Emily had two parents as it was, and now she was going to go out and get a third. *La-freaking-dee-da.*

"Yeah, I mean, I've Googled her before, but not very thoroughly. I'm going to be more methodical this time. I really think that finding her will help me ... accept all this," she said, trying to ignore Trix's blatant hostility.

"Or she could turn out to be a big disappointment who dates a guy with a giant squid tattoo."

When their order was called, Emily went up to get the food and saw, standing at the counter, Ryan McElvoy. Her heart giddyupped against her ribs.

"Hey, Lean Bean," he said, seeming genuinely happy to see her.

"Hey, Ryan," she answered, as nonchalantly as she could.

"What up?"

"Me," she said. "And lunch."

He broke into a full grin. "Nice," he said, nodding. He wore loose jeans and a Lucky Charms t-shirt that had been bleached almost beyond recognition.

Emily smiled and grabbed the tray holding her food. As she did, something caught her arm. Then, as if in stop motion animation, her lunch and Trix's went sliding sliding sliding across the tray, teetered, then dropped and crashed to the floor.

"Oh no," she cried, waiting for the burst of laughter that inevitably followed moronic spills like hers. She wasn't looking forward to it, but then she could at least bow, laugh at herself, and pick it all up.

Instead, there was silence.

Emily's face turned hot and she stooped, gathered the scattered French fries and ruined sandwiches.

Ryan crouched next to her and helped her pick up.

"Thanks," she muttered.

"No worries."

Trix called out, "Nice drop, klutzy girl." She clapped loudly until several others joined in. It seemed too late, though, to do the bowing shtick. So, Emily just waved weakly, shoved her tray in a bus tub and hurried out the front door.

"Hey, wait up," Trix called. "You're not mad are you? I was just trying to, you know, lighten the mood. God, you'd think you'd dropped a burning torch the way the place shut down."

"I'm not mad," Emily said, her stomach growling angrily. "Let's just get back to school."

"It wasn't a big deal, you know," Trix said.

"Right."

"At least you got Ryan's attention. He probably thought you did it on purpose."

Above them, seagulls circled, hoping for handouts.

Emily said, "Is that supposed to make me feel better?"

"I ... uh ... guess not. But it does make it funnier."

"Glad I'm so amusing." Emily strode ahead, her long legs easily covering more ground than Trix could hope to unless she skittered next to her like a small bird.

Emily pushed straight into the nearest bathroom and locked herself in a stall. Without pulling down her pants, she sat on the toilet. She studied the graffiti she'd seen a hundred times before. *Beth is a crackwhore. Andy + Daphne Forever!!! I hate Calculus.*

It calmed her, somehow, to read the scribbles. To know that girls in her class were so angry, so obsessed, so distraught that they had to express themselves with a ballpoint pen on metal walls.

What would she write? *Being six foot blows! Emily is an idiot! And she also can't stop thinking about Ryan McElvoy. She sometimes loves her best friend and sometimes hates her guts.*

That afternoon she avoided both Trix and Ryan in the hallways, taking alternate paths through the school to get to class. When the last bell rang, she filled her backpack with books as quickly as she could and dashed to her bike.

"Yo," Trix said, appearing out of nowhere. "You made yourself scarce today."

Emily bent low and jammed the key into her bike lock.

"I'm gonna go over to Sonic Boom and check out some tunes." Trix couldn't quite bring herself to ask Emily if she wanted to come. She figured Emily would tag along if she wanted to.

"Can't," Emily said. A cool rain started to fall, pinging her scalp. She pulled up her hood. "I have a quiz to study for."

Trix narrowed her eyes. "What class?"

"History."

Trix kept staring at Emily, eyes all squinty and suspicious. Then, just like that, she decided to believe her. "You go study," Trix said into the rain. "Be off with you."

As Emily pedaled, she glanced back once and saw Trix walking toward Market Street by herself.

19. MARJORIE

TRIX WAS GLAD to be inside, out of the windy rain. She trolled through the aisles of CDs, enjoying the musty smell of the old record store. She wasn't looking for anything in particular, but the home ec teacher had left early that day, closing the room, and Trix didn't want to go to her depressing trailer yet.

She flipped through some hardcore metal stuff. The fact that Emily hated it made it all the more fun to look at. She was reading liner notes to a Danzig disc when Marjorie King, a senior, came toward her. "Trix Jones, yeah?"

Tearing her eyes away from the CD, she said, "That's me." She moved to a new bin. Marjorie was the type who was always trying to be outrageous just for the sake of it. She loved to shock people. She wasn't authentic in her rebelliousness. Just superfluous.

Marjorie followed her. "Do you know who I am?"

"Um, Melanie Cook?"

"Marjorie. King. As if you didn't know."

Her presumptuousness turned Trix off. *Like everyone should know her name just because she had purple hair and dressed like a goth?* "Oh, then," Trix said sarcastically. "Nice to meet you."

Marjorie asked what music Trix was into. Without looking up, Trix rattled off some of her favorites.

"Cool," Marjorie said approvingly. "Fugazi? Old school punk?"

"Sure," Trix said, brightening a little.

"Hey, a bunch of us are going down to Golden Gardens. We have some good weed and a case, if you want to come."

"It's like forty-five degrees out."

"We won't feel it after a while."

Marjorie had a bull ring in her nose and three studs through her left eyebrow. Her face was freckled and her eyes rimmed in thick jet-black liner. "Nah," Trix said. "I'm not into braving the elements."

"What else you have going on?" Marjorie challenged.

This stopped Trix. Marjorie was right. She had a stifling trailer, a blaring TV, and a checked out mother. The only thing at all worth going home for was David. Though he would probably be roaming around outside or sleeping.

Trix shrugged. "All right." She dropped a CD back into place. "I'll go."

"Marcel's driving," Marjorie said. Marcel turned out to be the guy working behind the counter. They loitered around, waiting for his shift to end at four thirty, and when it did, he led them and two other guys Trix didn't recognize out to a beat-up minivan.

The ride to Golden Gardens, a beach in north Seattle, was cold and loud. Marcel blasted music that was a little too screamy even for Trix. At the parking lot they all spilled out. Sailboats bobbed and creaked along the piers. A few brave families and vagrants sat on the damp sand, facing the steel gray water.

Trix, Marjorie, and the rest of the group took a picnic table under the trees. Beers were handed out. A joint was lit and passed around. What seemed at first to have been a time-killing outing with a bunch of people Trix didn't care about, started to morph into something fun. Buzzed, the cold and drizzle didn't matter much. They sat in two tight lines along the table benches. Someone brought out a bag of pretzel rods, which, of course, turned into fodder for all sorts of dirty jokes and pantomimes.

Trix seemed to have a lot in common with Marjorie, who lived only with her mother. Marjorie's dad had died in a rodeo when she was young. Then she, her mom, and her twin little sisters had moved from Oklahoma up to Seattle.

"She dates these losers," Marjorie said, her eyes red-rimmed.

"Oh, my mom, too!" Trix crowed, telling everyone the story of Rodney and his ridiculous tattoo. It felt good to say it to people who understood. She always got the feeling that Emily thought Trix and her blue-collar problems were beneath her.

Trix lost count of the number of times the joint was passed to her. She drank a few beers and gobbled God knew how many pretzels.

For the first time in a long time, since she was a little kid maybe, she felt happy.

20. FOUND

EMILY SAT IN her room trying to study.

She read dates and battles and Chinese dynasties, but it was as dry as butterless toast.

Slamming her textbook shut with a satisfying thud, she went out into the hall where the family computer sat in the loft. Melissa had arranged dried flowers next to it that often shed and left crunchy bits all over the mouse pad.

Emily shook off the pad and clicked the machine out of its sleep.

She went to Facebook, which was becoming more of a habit.

There was a message waiting.

Hey Bean,

I'm sorry about what went down at lunch today. Please know I don't think any less of you for it. Happens to the best of us.

Ryan

P.S. I still would've eaten the fries.

She laughed out loud.

High on his contact, she Googled Marilyn Lucas, as she'd done a million times before. A lot of women who weren't her mother came up—a professor from Kansas, a Facebook profile that showed a girl with ginormous breasts spilling over the top and around the sides of a tank top, the owner of a pet spa in New York.

Emily typed in Marilyn Wozniak (her mother's maiden name) and got the usual stuff. Social networking links she'd already checked out and found not to be her mom.

This time, though, she searched with a fervor she hadn't before, until she got to page 24 and saw something. Something that made her suck in her breath and sit back in her chair.

A Marilyn Wozniak in Bisbee, Arizona. Emily clicked the link and was taken to the homepage of an art gallery. The background of the page was black and decorated with paintings of coyotes, front feet perched on logs, mouths open in long howls. Also, small owls looking out of cacti and fat gila monsters with skinny, red tongues.

There was a familiarity about the strokes, the style of the paintings, though Emily couldn't have pinpointed what. Then she thought of a picture that had hung in their old house on Earl, a seascape with whales and seals and starfish. As a younger kid, she'd never questioned where it had come from. It'd simply always been there. Now, though, she knew. Her mother had painted it.

She wondered where it was now.

Her heart beating faster, she clicked the link to go to Artists' profiles.

And there Marilyn was. In full color with a thin, drawn face, long, gray hair, bright eyes not quite focused on the camera, and the same high cheekbones as Emily and Kristen.

Emily jumped up, ran to her sister's room, and pounded on the door. No answer. Then she remembered Kristen's basketball game at Roosevelt.

"Oh my God," she muttered to herself. "Oh my God."

She sat back down to read Marilyn Wozniak's blurb:

"Marilyn Wozniak was born in 1962 in Pittsburgh, Pennsylvania. She studied at The School of Visual Concepts in Seattle, Washington. Since 2002, her art has been exhibited in several local galleries, as well as at Bernardo Kling in Santa Fe, New Mexico.

When she's not painting, she can be found in her garden, canning tomatoes, or reading in a hammock."

Oh, Emily thought. *Isn't that nice? Canning tomatoes. Reading in a hammock. What about helping raise the two daughters you gave birth to almost twenty years ago. What about them?*

"I hate you," she said to the ceiling. "I hate you."

She stared at her mom's picture. "I hate you."

Marilyn was a lanky woman. Even though the photo only showed the top half of her, you could tell.

Emily tried to imagine her dad with this Marilyn Wozniak and found she couldn't. As much as she hated to admit it, Melissa suited him well with her petite build and lust for fitness and health food. She was slowly converting him over to eating granola, rejecting red meat, and walking a few miles most nights.

What had Emily's father been like with her mother? More artistic? More free-spirited?

It was hard to picture her dad that way, with his perfectly creased Dockers, button-down oxfords, and bitter lines framing his thin lips.

In any case. *Mother of God.* Emily'd just found her mom. The woman of few snapshots and sparse memories. The woman who'd found it necessary to paint a celestial scene on the station wagon before leaving in it forever. The woman in whose uterus Emily had lived for the first nine months of her existence. The woman who'd missed her birthdays and taking Emily to get her ears pierced and teaching her how to make scrambled eggs.

After all these years of not knowing if Marilyn was alive or dead.

Mother of freaking God.

HER MOM WAS the first thing Emily thought of when she woke up the next morning. Marilyn. An artist in Bisbee, Arizona. Alive and seemingly well.

A chilly breeze blew in through the slender exposed strip of metal screen. Emily clenched the cotton jersey sheet in her hands and curved her body inward.

Anger and hope created a terrible steaming crater in her stomach. What should she do with her new information? Should she try to get in touch? Should she share it with Kristen or would it just upset her? Should she sit on the revelation and try not to think about it too much, try to go on with her life?

What was a 16-year-old girl supposed to do with such news?

Resentment flared, blotting out her excitement. Her mother put her in this situation. A situation she would've foreseen if she'd had any long-sightedness at all. Of course one or both of her daughters would try to find her someday. She couldn't have predicted the Internet, of course, but there were other methods, even that many years ago. Snail mail, for crying out loud. Phone calls.

The means didn't really matter, though. The fact was, Emily had located Marilyn and now she didn't, for the life of her, know what to do with that intelligence.

21. SHAKY ALLIANCE

"RYAN MCELVOY? HE'S a snooze. A boring prep."

"Really?" Trix said. "You think of him as preppy?"

"He's on the Stanford train, believe me. A total vanilla," Marjorie said.

They walked down the railroad tracks that snaked along the ship canal where fishing boats docked. It made Trix stupidly happy to hear Ryan described as a "total vanilla."

For once, her skin was calm as water on a still day, not at all itchy. She smoked her cigarette and tramped along, a salty breeze in her face.

They passed a homeless man pushing, through the mud, a grocery cart full of empty cans, a dirty sleeping bag, a bent bike wheel.

"You don't like McElvoy, do you?" Marjorie asked, kicking a beer bottle hard against a metal rail. It shattered and she laughed.

"No," Trix said. "Hell, no. But I think Emily does."

"Yeti?"

Irritation flared in Trix's gut. She and Emily weren't on the best terms right then, but it didn't mean Trix wanted people trashing her. "Her name's Emily."

"Oh, whoa! Didn't mean to diss your friend. She's vanilla too, by the way."

Emily wasn't, actually, vanilla. But she could be on the pious side.

Trix and Marjorie wandered down to the canal's edge and tossed their cigarette butts in. The water was greasy with oil and reflected the huge hulls of fishing boats that would soon be sailing up to Alaska.

"Who do you like?" Trix asked.

"Everyone," Marjorie said. "And no one. Which is to say, I'll sleep with anyone, but no one gets to have my heart."

Sad, Trix thought. But it was what she liked about Marjorie, too. There was something inaccessible about her. Something that could not be tamed.

"Ever?"

"Never."

Trix felt like a marshmallow compared to Marjorie. She knew she seemed tough on the outside, but her trampiness and anger hid the goo between her ribs.

"You're one of a kind, Marjorie King."

Marjorie laughed—a loud, joyous rumble. "I know."

They each lit new cigarettes and walked the steel rails of the tracks, balancing like little kids on beams, with their arms out. They slipped and laughed and got back up, both happy to have found someone to relate to. Neither knowing yet that this new friendship was going to take them places they shouldn't be treading.

22. FLYING SOLO

ONE EVENING, A few days before Halloween, Emily's dad and Melissa sat the girls down in the living room and announced they were going to Vancouver for the weekend. "A getaway we badly need," Melissa said.

A getaway from what? Emily wanted to ask. *All you do is hang around drinking smoothies and green tea and playing on your computer.* But, instead, Emily said, "That sounds nice."

"We trust we can leave you girls here alone for three nights," Bob Lucas boomed.

Kristen was replacing the laces on a pair of sneakers. "Of course."

Emily chimed in, "We'll only throw a couple of parties. With no more than three kegs each. Promise!"

Raising his eyebrows and shaking his head, her dad said, "We'll be calling every night."

She wondered if her dad had ever gone on weekend trips with her mom. Over to the Gorge or up into the mountains or the coast. Driving the famous getaway station wagon.

"We'll be good," Kristen said.

"As usual," Emily added.

"If anything comes up, you can always call Claudia," Melissa said. Claudia was a scarily fit, sixty-something woman who lived a couple blocks away. She was tan and sinewy, with pure white hair she wore pulled back into a high ponytail. Melissa sometimes ran with her.

"We'll have our cells, too," their dad reminded them.

Once the paranoid adults were satisfied they'd adequately prepared Emily and Kristen and secured the premises, they slipped from the room.

Emily and Kristen gave each other sidelong glances, trying not to break into huge smiles.

"PARTY!" TRIX LOUD-whispered between their classroom desks. She'd barely spoken to Emily in the past week, but when Emily announced her news, Trix had to make her case.

"No way," Emily said.

"Oh c'mon. When are you gonna get this chance again? Just a small one. Like, 50 people."

The room was cold, the sleeves of Emily's shirt too thin and too short. She could feel the desk's cool Formica under her arms.

She sensed Ryan three rows behind her. She could be in a stadium with thousands of people and she'd always know his coordinates in relation to hers.

She said, "You can't control how many people come to those things. Besides, no." Emily would be killed if her dad found out.

"You're wasting your opportunity. Big house. No parents. God. If only I could be so lucky."

It was then that Johnson came into the room.

Emily allowed herself one glance backward. Ryan's eyes were locked on her.

She whipped around toward the front, her heart pounding so hard she didn't know how she'd focus on what Mr. Johnson was saying, hoping, as she always did, that her intestines didn't make some horrible noise during that hour.

Thankfully, she was able to keep her body quiet and even take a few notes during class.

Mr. Johnson announced the Theater of the Absurd plays were due Monday and informed the class that some people would be reading theirs aloud.

As Emily got up to leave, there was a tug at her arm. It was Ryan. "I hear you and Kristen are flying solo this weekend."

They were in the hallway by then, a million kids zipping past. It smelled like cafeteria pizza.

"What? You already heard?" Emily said, biting her lip.

"You gonna go crazy?" He pushed his brown hair off his forehead and readjusted his backpack.

She realized as she stood there that their height difference was negligible if she slouched. This made her happy. She brushed away Melissa's voice in her head that hissed, *No one looks good stooped over.*

"Nah," Emily said, suddenly wishing she were planning to go a little crazy.

"Bummer. I'd like to see what Emily Lucas does with no supervision." A few people glanced at them, sizing up what this interaction between Ryan and Emily meant. Trix slid past, her eyebrows pulled inward, her lips curled in distaste.

The thought came to Emily in a flash, quicker than a droplet of water falling from faucet to sink: *Trix is jealous.*

Emily looked away quickly and focused on the boy in front of her.

"Oh, it's … " she faltered, trying to think of something clever to say, distracted by the fury in Trix's eyes. "It wouldn't be pretty. And anyway, I can't. The Theater of the Absurd project? I know you're done, but I haven't even started." *Brilliant, Einstein.* Her excuse was homework. She might as well wear a t-shirt that said, "World's biggest dork." Maybe she'd go to CafePress.com and have one made up.

He said, "Write it tonight."

She shrugged, knowing she'd totally blown the conversation.

As they moved apart, toward their separate classes, Ryan said, "You'll change your mind."

THAT NIGHT, EMILY sat down on her bed and pried off her boots, painfully aware that she had to finish her Theater of the Absurd play but wanting only to stare at the ceiling and think about her conversation with Ryan.

She let herself lay there for a few minutes, breathing in, breathing out. There were so many better things she could've said than what had actually come out of her mouth. Clever, witty non sequiturs that would've reeled Ryan in like a docile trout.

Then her mind began to flip through a half dozen scenarios during which she might run into him that weekend. A small get-together, maybe? On the lawn, no one allowed inside. No. No. She couldn't. A game—wasn't there football or something Saturday night? A meal—burgers at Dick's. A walk along the beach—or would it be too cold?

Finally, heaving herself off the bed and going to the computer out on the landing, she started typing a first act about two girls waiting for a phone call from a boy.

The assignment sucked her in and the next time she looked up at the monitor's clock, she saw an hour and a half had passed. She was just finishing the third page when Melissa trotted up the stairs. Cleaning her cell phone with a Clorox wipe, she said, "Hey. I'd rather Trix not come over while we're gone."

Emily stretched and twisted around to crack her back. "Why not?"

"Your dad and I don't ... completely ... trust her." Melissa must've seen Emily's hackles rising, because she said, "I know she's a good friend of yours. But, if you're going to hang out, could you just meet her somewhere else?"

"God," she said. "I never knew you didn't like my friends." Truthfully, she probably wouldn't have seen Trix anyway. Trix had been either working or hanging out with creepy Marjorie King every time Emily tried to reach out.

Melissa tossed the wipe into a trash can, her phone dangling from one hand. "It's not that we don't like her. We just don't think she has a good head on her shoulders like you do."

Emily thought "good head on your shoulders" was dumb phraseology. It always made her think of some neckless mutant. Maybe with one eye and no ears. She asked Melissa, "And do you ever think for yourself? Or is it all *We*?"

Melissa lowered her chin and raised her brows.

"Sorry," Emily said. "It's fine. I'll just spend the weekend alone."

Sighing, Melissa said, "C'mon, Em."

"Okay, okay. I'll suspend my social life while you're gallivanting around Canada."

"Oh, the drama," Melissa said.

Emily watched her move down the hall, petite frame swaying, black hair grazing her shoulders.

Gag.

She grabbed a bag of Fritos and a Diet Coke from a plastic grocery sack she kept stashed in her room, then went back to work, diving into her play with a vengeance. It wasn't even about the grade. Writing the assignment was offering her some sort of release, some way to channel all the stuff about Marilyn Wozniak. And also Ryan, Sam, and Trix. As if tiny lightning bolts of petulance and anxiety and anticipation were shooting from her fingertips and appearing onscreen.

And under it all ran the ticker that always accompanied her work: *Would this have made Marilyn proud? If she had a chance to read it, would it make her want to come back?*

23. Everyone Wants To Be Liked

TRIX HAD A plan. The most brilliant plan she'd hatched in a while. It would make her popular (which she had mixed feelings about, but still), increase Marjorie's respect for her, and get her noticed by the guys she wanted to notice her. Namely, Ben, Devlin, and Ryan McElvoy. It would bring her closer to her sparkly new life.

She'd thought of it that afternoon as she sat at one of the sewing machines in the home ec room after school.

She was going to throw a party at Emily's house. A fantastic bash that would put her on everyone's social map. She wasn't supposed to care about such things, she knew. Part of her, in fact, disdained calculated efforts to sway public opinion. But then there was the other part of her. The part that wanted to be liked.

She couldn't let Emily find out ahead of time, of course. It was going to be a surprise. So, on Friday afternoon, Trix breezed into the school computer lab and logged into her Facebook account. From there, she posted an event: Party at Emily Lucas's house, 2512 Asher St. NW, tonight at 8pm. She sent it to all her "friends" at CHS, then sent a mass email to everyone else she could think of.

She invited Sam, who she was hoping would somehow thwart Ryan from Emily's path. She knew, from there, word would spread like dandelions through a meadow.

Then she went home to get ready.

Her mother sat on the couch, as usual, watching some crime drama while feeding David nibbles of microwave popcorn. "Mom!" Trix said. "He can't eat that stuff."

"What?" her mom said, without taking her eyes off the screen. "Why not?"

"I don't know. What if he chokes on a kernel or something?" She scooped David up and took him into her room where he sat on her dresser and watched her change. She picked out a tight tank top, a fitted cotton jacket with big rolled cuffs and black leggings. She wore the giant hoop earrings she always had on and her wedge boots.

She was ready to rock.

24. BAD SCENE

EATING A BOWL of ramen noodles, Emily stood at the counter flipping through *Shape* magazine (Melissa's). It was boring. Energy drink ratings. Healthy meal recipes. Workouts. And the cover model looked like she'd gotten lost on her way to a Cosmo shoot.

Darkness pressed against the windows like waxed paper, raindrops occasionally pelting the glass. Kristen was staying at her friend Karissa's, so Emily was alone.

When she finished her noodles, she flicked on the stereo and found some Chairlift. She wanted to call Trix, just to see what she was doing, to alleviate the loneliness a little. But Trix had been acting so weird. Plus, she didn't want to have to tell Trix she wasn't allowed in the house.

Emily set the magazine back on the stack of unopened mail and decided she would go online for a while.

She was taking the stairs two at a time when someone knocked on the front door. Less of a knock really, and more of a fist pound.

She paused, not knowing if she should answer.

"It's me, Em!" Trix's muffled voice called. "Let me in, I'm getting soaked out here!"

She strode to the door and pulled it open. Even though she wasn't supposed to, she had to invite Trix in. Trix, who was dripping like a kitten that'd been found face first in a mud puddle. Maybe she was there to talk about things and explain why their friendship had seemed so strained lately. Or maybe they'd just hang out like old times, fighting over music and forgetting about the tension between them.

Trix pulled off her ratty leopard-print coat and let it slide to the floor. She grabbed a hank of her hair and squeezed. "It's dumping."

"I know."

Water streaked Trix's face like tears, dripped off her lashes. Her eyes widened. "Let's invite some people over."

"No!" Emily said. "God, my dad—"

"What he doesn't know … "

"I can't invite people over."

"Well," Trix said. "You can't, but I can."

Emily heard a rustling outside the door and another pound. She swallowed hard and swung it open. A couple of guys from school, Isaac O'Leary, Adam Williams, Marjorie King, and three freshman girls stood there. Isaac wore a gorilla mask pushed up on top of his head and one of the girls had a devil's ear headband. Emily glared at Trix, trying to imperceptibly shake her head.

Trix pretended not to see. The look on Emily's face when Isaac, Adam, and Marjorie had come in was classic. "Just, you know, an intimate gathering. A pre-Halloween soirée."

Emily considered turning them away, into the dark rain. But then, how lame would that make her seem? So, okay, Trix plus six kids. She could get away with that, probably, clean up really well after they left. Keep the curtains closed so Claudia wouldn't notice.

Emily said, "I don't have beer or anything. Like, 7Up is the hardest stuff in the house." She wasn't about to get into her dad's microbrews.

Everyone looked at Adam who held a case of Pabst Blue Ribbon.

Defeated, she stood back and let them enter. She pointed to the family room off the kitchen, but grabbed Trix's arm. "Are you that desperate?" she hissed.

Small flames burned where Trix's eyes should've been. "I want word to get back to the Trifecta of Farkette Dunces that fun was had by all, and they weren't invited." That was Trix's excuse, and she was sticking to it.

Emily's hand flew to her mouth. "How many people did you tell?"

"A few others. Don't worry so much. It'll be fine." She shook free of Emily's grip, wanting to tell her to grow up, and followed the others to the back of the house.

Emily could hear beer cans popping open. The music's volume went up. She wished Kristen were home. She'd know what to do, how to handle this situation without pissing anyone off or getting herself in deep trouble.

As Emily started to make her way to the others so she could lay down ground rules, the doorbell rang. She groaned. When she answered it, she saw the blond boy Trix had hooked up with at Jason Bleak's party. He had four or five guys with him and held a bottle of gin. It wasn't until Ben Mason showed up, someone Trix had gone out with for a few weeks and really liked, but who'd dumped her, that Emily realized what Trix was doing. Not only was she using Emily to throw Cannon High School's biggest off-the-hook party of the year, but she was trying to play guys off each other to get attention.

"Trix!" Emily called, looking through the rooms. But there were so many people by then that finding her was impossible.

Above all the other heads Emily spotted Sam standing by the gas fireplace with Jason Bleak, drinking from a small, brown jug. How'd he sneak in?

She scrambled around the house, moving fragile lamps and vases to higher ground, hiding Melissa's laptop, and locking doors. At one point she grabbed duct tape from the garage and wrapped some around the front of the refrigerator to keep people out.

Her stomach had knotted into an anxious, tumor-like mass.

When it all became too much, she realized she needed air, to get away from the music and smell of alcohol. She burst outside, where clusters of kids stood smoking. The rain had stopped, but a healthy wind still whipped everyone's hair around their heads, and jackets around their hips. Emily held her skull, frantic. "Crap," she muttered to herself. "Crap, crap, crap."

She folded her long body so she was sitting on the curb and wondered how soon before a neighbor called the cops. She sat like that for a long time, vaguely aware of the music thumping from inside, intermittent laughter, and the smell of cigarettes.

Then she heard, "Doesn't look to me like you're studying so hard."

She saw a pair of sneakers. She raised her eyes. Jeans. Gray zip sweatshirt. Face. Ryan's. "It's all Trix," Emily said. "And I'm so completely screwed."

He lowered himself next to her. She noticed he didn't carry a six-pack or a fifth and was grateful. "I'm such a cliché," she said. "Such a pathetic cliché. It's like a bad high school movie. Teenage girl gets bullied into throwing a giant party. People have sex in the bedrooms," she felt her face flush as she said this, "and trash the house and girl has to work for decades to earn back her parents' trust. Not to mention send them her first gazillion paychecks after she graduates to pay for the damage."

"Just call the police," Ryan said.

"What?"

"Yeah. The party will get busted up, everyone'll leave and you still come off as having hosted a kick-ass shindig."

The sour, earthy smell of marijuana curled and dipped its way around her.

"But then it's on, like, our permanent record or something. I mean, will I get a ticket? Will my dad find out about it?"

Ryan's bent head was close to Emily. She inhaled the scent of him: washed cotton and something faintly evergreen. "It's better," he said, "than your dad finding out because the house is a smoldering pile of ashes in the middle of the lot."

She felt overwhelmed. Totally out of her league.

"I'm not trying to scare you," he said, looking back at the house. "But this party is getting huge. And Bleak's house was so completely thrashed by his throwdown that his parents took his car keys for the rest of the year."

Emily didn't have her license yet, but she knew her dad would think up an equally stunting punishment.

At that moment, she saw April, Kennedy, and Vanessa standing in her driveway, holding beer cans, other kids weaving around them.

"The Farkettes," she said and stood. She stepped on and off the curb, trying to decide her next course of action. It was then that the side door whooshed open.

Trix strode across the driveway, her curly hair bouncing over her shoulders. Even from there, Emily could see her mouth set in an angry line. She busted in on the Farkettes's circle. "Excuse me! Hello? Excuse me! Were you invited to this party? Because I'm pretty sure I didn't notify any of you."

April, a hand stuck casually in her jeans pocket, her head tossed back irreverently, said, "Ben told us about it."

Emily could almost hear Trix's jaw crack as she ground her teeth. "Ben Mason," she said, nodding and taking a backward step. She knotted her arms over her chest.

"The one and only," April said, a smile tugging at the corners of her mouth.

Someone in the crowd yelled, "Ben and April are banging."

Everyone laughed. Everyone except Emily, Ryan, and Trix.

A rushing sound like an enormous wave filled Trix's ears.

She growled to April, "I have two words for you: consolation prize."

April came back with, "I have three words for you, Movin' on Up."

More laughter.

"All right!" Emily called, hands cupped around her mouth. "This party's over! Everyone get out. Go do your drinking and trash talking in an alley or something!"

Trix flashed her a look that could've liquefied a brick wall.

"Are you freaking kidding me?" someone said.

"Over! Time to go!" Emily yelled.

Furious, Trix went up to Emily and said, "What are you doing?"

"Shutting this thing down, Trix."

"It's not yours to shut down."

Emily actually cackled. A cold breeze rippled through her hair. A cold breeze tinged with the scent of beer and far off burning leaves and teen spirit. "It's my house."

Trix's eyes were wild, her teeth bared. "You can't," she said. "Don't, Em. Don't do it." Nothing had gone how it was supposed to. They hadn't even gotten to the good part of the night.

Emily couldn't quite believe Trix's recklessness. She certainly was no shrinking violet, but this exploit? It was over the top.

Just then, a red Honda Civic Emily recognized as Kristen's friend Karissa's car pulled up along the curb. Kristen jumped out and jogged across the lawn. "Emily? What is this?"

Emily looked up the street. It was barren. Quiet except for this house and the wind that howled through the trees. She sighed. She turned to Kristen and said, "Help me."

Together, Emily, Kristen, and Ryan made their way through the yard and into the house, calling that the police were coming and to get out fast.

Kids scattered like ants away from a smoking cigarette butt.

Engines started in unison. Many people just wandered off down the street, still with beers in hand. A few disappeared out the back, hopping fences.

There were some stragglers lingering inside the house, still talking and laughing in the kitchen. A guy and a girl Emily didn't recognize canoodled at the top of the stairway. She broke them up with a loud, "Take it to Motel 6."

Trix found Marjorie and they convened on the front porch with Adam and Isaac. Unexpectedly, Sam was still there, lingering. Marjorie said, "This is so effing lame. I thought it was supposed to be awesome."

"It was," Trix said, heat creeping up her chest and flooding her cheeks. How dare Emily make Trix look stupid in front of her new friend. The only friend who really understood her. "Emily just doesn't know how to party."

"Clearly." Marjorie lit a cigarette and sat down on the wooden steps. Following her lead, everyone else perched on the stairs or railing, too.

"So, what do we do now?" Adam asked.

Marjorie yelled, "Will you let me smoke this before we decide? Christ!"

Pushing back her curls with shaking hands, Trix said, "Let's go get hammered somewhere. I'm done with this place."

25. CLEANUP IN AISLE EMILY

EMILY DIDN'T SEE where Trix had gone, but finally the place was empty except for Kristen, Ryan, and herself. Stunned, she swept bottle caps from the table into her palm. "What a mess," she said.

Kristen carried the recycling bin through the rooms, tossing in heavy glass bottles and crumpled cans. "Will you please explain to me how that started?"

The party had spread like flames across a dry prairie. Emily had never experienced anything like it. "It wasn't my fault, okay? Word just got around." Despite her fight with Trix, she was reluctant to tell Kristen that Trix had been the mastermind.

Some rap song still played on the stereo at low volume. Emily punched it off.

She closed rifled-through cupboards and scrubbed the sticky kitchen counters with a sponge.

Ryan had gone onto the back deck where he was righting lawn furniture. She walked out after him, the cold wind grabbing her. She said, softly, "You don't have to do this."

"I want to."

All the lights in the house were on and they made a pattern of yellow rectangles across the deck and grass. The cold air bordered on bitter. "But, why? All your friends are somewhere else."

He turned a metal chair and replaced Melissa's red, floral cushion. "You're not somewhere else."

Emily's heart fluttered, like someone erratically pounding a bongo drum. "Well," she said. "Thank you."

She maneuvered so she was one step down from him, her feet firmly planted on the ground. Ryan edged closer. When he got so he stood in front of her, they were the same height.

Her heart and breath and thoughts clanged. She could smell him again, that cottony, evergreen scent. Oh my God, she thought. Ryan McElvoy. Ryan McElvoy. There is his neck, his pointy Adam's apple, his skin a little stubbly. And there's his chin, kind of square and solid. There's his mouth, his lips a peachy purple in this light and they're coming closer. Closer. Closer.

Then, standing on different levels so they were perfectly aligned, with wind spinning the bamboo chimes and rattling the window screens, the house lit like a jack-o'-lantern, and the sound of the clinking bottles that Kristen was collecting inside, Ryan McElvoy kissed Emily. And his mouth was warm, and it was good.

When they pulled apart, she realized she'd been clutching the sleeve of Ryan's hoodie. She looked up at him and all she could think to say was, "I'm glad you stayed." He felt so foreign next to her. Such an oddly different species, the attractive male. But also inviting and intoxicating. More than anything, she wanted to stand there and keep kissing him. Or, better yet, move him inside where it was warm.

She knew they couldn't exactly start making out while Kristen cleaned the house, though, so she swallowed hard and smiled.

Ryan smiled back. "You have soft lips," he said.

Emily's smile grew, though she was equal parts embarrassed and flattered.

A stinging raindrop hit her forehead, then a second and third. She couldn't help but wonder if this kiss would've happened had she been standing on the upper step. Her voice was almost a whisper when she asked, "Why me?"

He chuckled, pulled his hand down over his mouth, and rested it on his chin. "Because," he said, his voice dipping, then coming back up, as if that one word should convey the reason he'd chosen her. "You're you. There's no other Lean Bean."

She wished Ryan wouldn't call her that, but to him she supposed it meant something endearing. To her, it was just a reminder of her height.

She said, "Let's finish this up before we get drenched."

He agreed and they jogged around the front of the house to pick up the detritus that'd been left there. What they found were a group of people sitting on the porch steps.

Leaning back on her elbows, oblivious to the rain that had started, Trix took short, nervous drags from a cigarette. Marjorie King and Sam perched next to her. "There you are," Sam said.

Emily stopped short, her goofy smile and the contented, exhilarated hum emanating from her extinguished.

She shifted her attention from Sam to Trix. She walked up so the toes of her Chuck Taylors almost touched the toes of her friend's platform boots. "What was that?" she asked.

Trix's eyes were red, but it wasn't clear if they were red because she was trying to hold back tears or from the smoke drifting into them.

Trix wanted nothing to do with Emily right then. She'd ruined everything. If the night had gone as Trix planned, she'd be deciding between Devlin, Ben, and Ryan. Instead, Ryan stood there, his fingers linked loosely with Emily's, both so self-satisfied they practically glowed.

"Trix?"

"What?" her tone was flat. Dead. She looked up at Emily, daring her to lecture.

"What's going on with you?" Emily wished more than anything that Sam, Marjorie, and the others would go. They had nothing to do with this. And besides, Sam kept staring and was making her supremely uncomfortable.

The leaves that were still left in the trees above them swished and swashed dramatically. Every so often a full moon peeked from behind dark, fast moving clouds.

"What's going on with *you*?" Trix asked angrily.

Emily took a step back. "Me?"

"Yeah, you. Miss Prim. Miss Oh-no-I-couldn't-possibly-have-a-party-at-my-house. When did you get so boring?"

Ryan and Emily exchanged a look. His was unreadable but he offered a slight nod.

"Look," Emily said. "I'm not the one who's changed here. You are. Putting me on the spot like that was totally uncool. Totally thoughtless and selfish."

Trix crushed her cigarette under the heel of her boot. "That's me," she said. "Thoughtless and selfish."

Marjorie hooted into the night.

Emily tasted something sour, slightly bitter, in the back of her throat and imagined it seeping out her nostrils and the corner of her mouth. She didn't understand where Trix's resentment came from and why it was directed at her. Why was Trix so angry just because Emily was trying to do the right thing? "It doesn't *have* to be you."

Trix stood. "Yeah it does. It's my legacy. I'm outta here," she said. "Have fun with your boy-o. Enjoy it while you can. They all only want one thing."

Marjorie dropped a burning cigarette on the porch step and crushed it with her heel. Sam loped after them, turning back to raise one big hand. As they moved down the street under the orange sodium lights, Emily remembered how jealous and enraged Trix had looked coming out of Johnson's class earlier that day.

"She's a real treat," Ryan said, watching them go.

Emily wondered if Trix was jealous of Ryan, per se, or just that someone was paying attention to Emily at all. She was dumbfounded, too. Trix should've been falling all over herself apologizing, explaining, begging forgiveness. Instead she'd treated Emily like *she'd* done something wrong. "She … " Emily stopped, then started again. "She didn't used to be like that."

Ryan's hand slid up under her hood and rested there. Warmth coursed through her veins and she turned, intentionally slouching so their mouths could meet, and kissed him. A long kiss that pulled her tongue out to meet his and brought her hands up to his broad, boney shoulders.

It was absolutely nothing like Sam's slimy kiss.

This was restrained and electrifying. This was Ryan's mouth on Emily's. This was fantastically incredible.

She tried not to let herself wonder if they would kiss tomorrow and the next day, or if this was a one-night thing. She hoped it wasn't. God, she hoped it would go on.

26. FUN HOUSE

THEY WERE IN someone's apartment. Isaac's? The music was good. Loud and electric. Trix had drunk more than a six-pack on her own. And maybe vodka. She wasn't sure. She just knew she felt so good so good so good. Her head was on some guy's lap as he played air guitar and she tried not to fall asleep. She didn't want to miss any fun.

Marjorie lay on the floor and stared at the ceiling as if a movie played up there. She'd done something more than alcohol or weed, but Trix didn't know what.

Other people were around, too, but to Trix they moved like ghosts. She was focused on Marjorie. "Whatcha see up there?" she said. Her words sounded mushy even to herself.

Marjorie only laughed.

The song ended and the guy playing air guitar went limp. He stroked Trix's hair, saying something about how much of it there was and that it was like snarled weeds.

When he caught on a tangle, he ripped through it savagely.

Trix shrieked. The guy chuckled.

Fun house. That was kind of what this was like. Things loomed large and then small. A tangle in her hair was a big deal, then faded to nothing. Marjorie with all her makeup and black and purple hair seemed clownishly large, and then remote and tiny.

"Marj?" Trix said.

"Don't ever call me that!"

"Okay, um, Marjorie. I feel really strange. Like, more than beer and vodka strange."

Marjorie cackled again.

As if she were looking through a magnifying glass, Trix had a huge thought: Marjorie spiked one of her drinks with something. With some drug.

The party at Emily's, even though it had only been a few hours before, seemed far away now, like a farm on the distant horizon. What had been a major catastrophe earlier—the demise of her great plan to get attention—didn't matter at all anymore.

Suddenly, with the guy's skinny fingers traveling her scalp, she inhaled sharply. Her ideas, which had been so big they filled the room, shrunk to the size of a gumdrop. A grain of sugar on a gumdrop. He was looking for something in her hair. Bugs? Coins? Pills?

Trix knew she didn't want him to find whatever was in there.

She scurried over to Marjorie. She shook her shoulder. "We have to get out of here!" she said. She gave the guy a sidelong glance, knowing he was holding a handful of her strands. Oddly, she felt no pain.

"What?" Marjorie said slowly. "Why? I'm soooo happy right here."

"Because!" Trix was frantic. "We just have to."

"Relax and enjoy this."

"Enjoy what? Being picked at like a baboon?"

"The little gift I've given you," Marjorie said, her syllables slurred.

Sitting back on her haunches, Trix held her head in her hands. "Oh, Marjorie, what did you do?"

27. FADING TO BLACK

EMILY SAT AT the computer, alternately clicking every link related to Marilyn Wozniak and chatting with Ryan on Facebook. It seemed that overnight they were an item. Ryan was typing the word *We* a lot. *We should grab burgers. We have to get tix for the XY show at the Crocodile. When are we going camping at the Gorge?*

Every time she read that word, *We*, elation almost lifted her out of her creaky chair and flew her over Ballard, across Seattle, and above the roiling, cold Puget Sound. But the thing was, she was too afraid it wouldn't last to really enjoy it. She worried Ryan would come to his senses any second, slap his forehead and say, "Emily Lucas? What the bleep was I thinking?" She worried that her growth would deter him. A couple more inches and he'd be as good as gone.

So she kept her responses low key. *Sure, burgers are good. XY is in January, hold off on buying tix. Camping? Don't I need a sleeping bag for that?* Etcetera.

When he asked what else Emily was doing online, she replied vaguely. Browsing around. Listening to music. Which she was.

She kept checking for emails from Trix. Even a short note that said she was sorry. That she didn't know what had gotten into her. There was nothing, though.

Emily knew in her bones Trix was upset that Emily had, for the moment, gotten Ryan's attention. But, frankly, she wasn't going to apologize for that.

For years Emily had watched Trix get guy after guy. Many of them, without a doubt, had gone after her for the wrong reasons. But there'd been a few nice ones who'd crushed on her, too.

Now it was Emily's turn. She and Ryan connected and Emily wasn't about to hand him over to Trix on a silver platter. Not that he was the type to let himself be handed anywhere.

And after how Trix behaved the night before, Emily's motivation to spackle this nick, or more accurately this gaping hole, in their friendship, was zero. If Trix wasn't the one to come forward, Emily didn't know that it was reparable.

Ryan asked if anything in the house had broken during the party. She said no, but that she'd had to mop the sticky kitchen floor and mist some houseplants that'd taken a dousing of beer.

His interest was sweet. And every time Emily remembered his lips on hers, the warmth of his hand under her hood, the way he'd driven off a little before midnight, grinning and calling out his open window that she should get to work on her Theater of the Absurd play, she felt a rush of pleasure and heat deep in her chest.

Later, after they'd both signed off Facebook, Emily discovered a people finder site into which she typed her mother's name and, just like that, up popped her address and phone number. Emily could hardly believe how easy it was and that she hadn't tried it before.

There was Marilyn Wozniak in Bisbee, living on an actual street, with an actual 10-digit number that Emily could dial right that second and possibly hear her mom's voice. Not that she would. Heck no. The thought terrified her.

Under the column Related People, were Emily's grandparents' names and also Winslow Kratt.

Winslow Kratt?

Emily Googled him. He was shockingly easy to find. He appeared to be a gallery owner in Bisbee.

It occurred to Emily that her mother might be remarried, might even have other children. A new family.

She felt dizzy and cradled her forehead in her hands. The thought of her mother making chocolate chip cookies and buying clothes for other kids, kids who were not Kristen or her, made Emily physically ill.

Suddenly, all Trix's drama and the wonderfulness with Ryan faded to black. It was as if Marilyn's face hung in the sky like a moon, smudging out everything else. And that was when Emily started to scheme.

28. REVEAL

SATURDAY NIGHT EMILY and Ryan met up at India Bistro where they gorged themselves on *Saag Aloo* and *Naan*.

She couldn't help thinking, over and over, *So this is what it's like. This is what it's like to want a boy and to have him want you back and to go on a date and to sit across from the boy eating and flirting. This is what it's like.*

She knew it sounded cliché, but she feared she'd wake up. A couple of times she cupped a hand over the ivory votive to reassure herself that she was awake, to bring her skin a little too close to the hot flame.

Leaning against the back wall of the restaurant, she looked around at the plain trapezoidal room, at the few colorful cloths hanging from beige walls and candles flickering on tables. She felt content. But not yet safe. She wondered how much Ryan knew, or guessed, about her family situation. It seemed important, suddenly, to fill him in and let him decide if it was a deal-breaker or not.

"So," she said. "There's something I should tell you."

"Uh oh," he swallowed a bite and took a sip of tea. "What's that?"

"I've been on sort of a mission lately. Do you know my dad is married to someone who isn't my mother?"

"I kind of assumed that, yeah."

This barbed Emily a little. But, of course he'd assume that. Melissa, with her petite frame and sleek black bob, clearly wasn't her real parent.

Spinning the warm base of the candleholder around and around, she said, "My mom took off when I was four. I barely remember her. Just little fragments here and there. Lately I've been wanting to find her. And I did. Online I mean."

"Wait," he said, leaning over the table and drilling his warm blue eyes into Emily's. "You haven't even known where your mom is since you were four?"

"No, she took off and never looked back."

"Jeez, Bean."

"I know." Emily's heart beat hard. "I figured out she lives in Arizona. I have her contact info and everything. And I think I want to get in touch."

"That's huge," Ryan said, linking his fingers with Emily's over the tabletop. His hand felt meaty, knuckley, like a boy's.

Relief washed over her. He wasn't acting disturbed, like her announcement was TMI. He was doing exactly what she hoped he would: intently listening.

He added, "Let me know if I can help in any way."

Emily smiled at him. She appreciated his offer but knew opening communication with her long-lost mother was going to require every ounce of strength Emily possessed. And she had to do the legwork by herself.

Back out on the cold sidewalk, tugging their jackets around their middles, Ryan said, "You're not one to pick at your food, are you?"

Emily laughed. "How do you think I grew so much?"

After a few moments of walking and grinning, hands in their pockets, Ryan said, "So I had this idea."

"Shoot."

"Dave Eggers is doing a reading at Elliot Bay Books tonight. Wanna go? It's free."

And just like that, Emily felt like an insider, a girl swooning over a boy who liked her back, and she said, "That sounds … amazing."

AFTER THE READING, he drove her in his mom's light green Volkswagen bug, which he hated and called The Kiwi, through Pioneer Square, under wet trees that had lost most of their leaves, past Pike Place Market and on up to Ballard, their Seattle neighborhood that, though full of new condos and cool restaurants, was a huge hub of commercial fishing vessels and still retained a grittiness that appealed to Emily.

She thought of the last 24 hours as if it were a cheesy TV montage: his helping her at the party, online chatting, Indian food, and the Dave Eggers reading all sliding through her mind in slo-mo, with some Coldplay song in the background. She almost laughed, but held it together, hoping she just looked happy. Or maybe, coolly satisfied.

Her house was dark, looming, and lonely. Wordlessly, he walked her up to the door.

Emily thought it was probably some time after eleven, but she didn't want to look. "Are you ... do you want to hang out some more?"

"I'm supposed to be home by midnight," he said. He drew his thick brows together regretfully. His hands were stuffed in his pockets. His profile, as he looked down the row of houses on her street, was strong, almost exaggerated with his long, straight nose and jutting chin. "We can't let an empty house go to waste though, right?"

"That would be blasphemous." She unlocked the door and darted through the living room, turning on lights. She put on some chill music, good backgroundy stuff, and asked Ryan if he wanted anything to eat or drink.

He'd taken off his coat and laid it across the back of Melissa's favorite, red leather chair. He stood in the light of an iron floor lamp and said, flippantly, "Just you."

Emily laughed delightedly, nervously. They met at the sofa and began to kiss. They kissed in a way they hadn't before, opening their mouths wide and reaching desperately with their tongues. She buried her fingers in his hair, pulling his head to her, liking the small growls coming from the back of his throat.

They went on like that for a while, their bodies moving rhythmically to the thump of the tunes, devouring each other's faces and necks. And then Ryan's hands began to travel. Down her spine and up her shirt. She breathed in sharply, then exhaled in a long, low mewl of pleasure.

His palms skimmed over her bra strap several times and then, finally, lingered there.

"Where are you going with that?" Emily asked, her lips moving under his.

He pulled back and looked at her. "I don't know yet. Where do you want me to go with it?"

"I don't know yet."

"I can wait," he said.

She separated from him, shifting back and straightening her shirt. "Answer me this," she said. "Do you really like me, or are you just in this to nail the tall chick? Win some sort of bet."

He clasped his hands and let them hang between his knees. "Did you really just ask me that?"

"I think I did," she said, regretting it. She fully expected him to stand and go for his coat.

He didn't, though. He scooched slightly away, an ironic smile on his lips. "Want to watch TV or something then? Because I'd hang with you whether or not you put out, okay? I mean, I want to kiss you. I want to do more. But I don't have to. I like you, Emily. I like you a lot. More than I should."

"How much ... should you?" Emily said, all of her swelling–her throat, her heart, her nether regions.

"I shouldn't like you so much that it drives me insane," he said.

"You seem like the most sane person I know."

"I used to be very sane."

"Not anymore?"

"Not lately, no."

Emily walked over to the floor lamp and clicked it off, then rejoined Ryan on the couch.

She had no idea how far she'd let this go. She really liked him, of course. In fact, it was safe to say she was seriously infatuated. But she didn't want to become Trix either, giving it out too fast. Also, there was some part of her, a tiny fleck, worried that once she'd given away her body, she wouldn't be able to stop.

They stretched out next to each other and it was lovely because her height barely mattered and their bodies were pressed together and he held the back of her head as they kissed. And then his hand trailed up her spine again and she shivered with pleasure. His fingers went to her bra strap and, deftly, he popped it open.

Emily felt exposed and sexy and a little scared. But she let him go on.

He went around to the front then and touched her nipples with his fingertips. He squeezed gently, traced a circle around them, watching her the whole time, his eyes asking, *Is this okay?*

Almost imperceptibly, she nodded.

Slowly, so slowly she almost couldn't bear it, he cupped one breast and then the other. His own breathing, she noticed, had accelerated.

That was when she felt it. The hardness under his jeans. It thrust into her thigh like a small baseball bat and she didn't know what to do with it. Touch it? Look at it? Let it be?

"You did that," he said and chuckled.

"How?" she asked, all middle-school innocence. Except that she was sixteen and should definitely not play dumb. Or fish for compliments.

Instead of answering, a small groan escaped him.

They groped each other for what felt like ten minutes, but turned out to be an hour and a half. When Ryan glanced up at the clock he said, "Aw, crap." He rubbed his face and sat, his elbows on his knees.

"It's late," Emily said.

"Curfews blow."

"They suck in the worst way." She fervently wished they were in college, with no one accounting for where they were. She wanted Ryan to stay. She wanted to fall asleep with him beside her.

He waited there for several minutes, sitting quietly. "Okay," he said. "I guess I should head out."

Emily scrambled to hook her bra, then walked him to the door, the wood floor cold under her bare feet.

Ryan took a deep breath of the cool night air.

She didn't want him to leave, and was about to voice this, but was hit, now that they were upright and he was leaving, by a vulnerable feeling she felt she should subdue. "Well, I'll see you Monday, right?"

"Monday?" he said.

"Yeah. You know, school."

"Right," he nodded. "School."

He kissed her once more and Emily kept her eyes open. She saw the sweep of his dark lashes against his skin, the concavity of his cheeks, a largish ear.

"Bye, Ryan." She sounded, to herself, like a sad little girl and it disgusted her. Which caused her to turn her back to him quickly and slip inside.

The music, she'd noticed, had stopped. The house was quiet. Too quiet. She didn't feel like flipping through the iPod for more songs, so she went upstairs. It was late and she knew she should go to bed. Restless energy wouldn't let her, though. She went to Kristen's room and watched Ryan's mom's car recede down her street.

She prowled her way to the computer and brought it out of its slumber. Her plan was to search for more on Marilyn Wozniak and Winslow Kratt. But she ended up opening Word and working on her play.

She wrote until after three and, exhausted, shut everything down and went to bed. She had to cover her head with a pillow to block out the howl of the autumn wind.

29. NONPARENT NUMBER 1

TRIX WOKE WITH a headache the size of Mt. Rainier. She was relieved, though, to find she was in her own bed with no one except David the cat next to her. She tried to stay in that twilit consciousness, moving in and out of dreams where the throbbing in her temples was only a vague thud.

Sadly, her mom and Rodney the Octopus Man weren't cooperating. They murmured from the pull-out couch just on the other side of the wafer-thin wall. Their words were indecipherable, but the tone of the conversation was clipped and angry.

Reality imposed itself like an old-school TV coming to life— colors brightening, sound slowly amplifying.

David stretched out next to her, his ears flattening and his paws reaching for her face. He rested them gently on her cheek, claws retracted. The pads on the bottom of his feet were warm and he purred. She thought maybe if she just stayed in bed with him forever she could be happy. Just her and a vibrating cat and, in another part of the house, the promise of her mother dumping a loser boyfriend.

She had no idea how she'd gotten home after Marjorie had slipped Ecstasy into her beer. And that scared Trix. She wasn't afraid of getting a little out of control, going somewhat crazy, but when she lost whole hours with no memory of what had happened, this bugged the ratbones of out of her.

She hated not knowing what she'd done or said. Or who she might have given too much to.

Scratching David's belly, she burped. It tasted like beer.

Rodney's voice ratcheted into a loud crack.

Trix jumped.

Her mom yelled that if he didn't like the way she lived her life, he could get out.

"Oh, that's it then? It's your way or the highway?" Rodney roared.

"I have a *daughter* to protect!"

What a laugh. Trix didn't even have a curfew. She pushed her earbuds in and buried her face in David's soft stomach. She didn't need this this morning.

An hour later, after Rodney stormed out and all seemed to be quiet and relatively safe, Trix tiptoed to the bathroom for some ibuprofen. Her mom was in there doing a breathing treatment.

"Rodney's gone." Trix stated, her voice raspy.

"Yeah, thank God," her mom said around her plastic tube.

Trix popped two generic Advils and swallowed them with a handful of water.

"When'd you come in?" her mom asked. "You look like death warmed over."

"Feel like it, too."

"What'd you do?" her mom asked, looking suddenly concerned.

"Cigarettes, beer, and drugs."

Fiona laughed, thinking Trix was kidding.

Trix said, "Seriously," but it was lost in her mother's laughter-turned-hacking-cough. So Trix left the bathroom and made herself an enormous pot of coffee. She kind of wanted her mom to know about her destructive behavior. To stop her. To tell her she was worth more than that. But Trix also knew that a heartfelt self-esteem boost was not how Fiona would handle the matter. There would be screaming and door slamming and an attempted grounding that would never be enforced. Trix just didn't have the energy for a scene like that.

She thought about texting Emily and telling her what happened, that she was suddenly not so sure about Marjorie. She could imagine Emily's reaction, too, though. She'd sneer at her phone and be further convinced Trix was not good enough people for her. *Trashy Trix*, she'd think. *I'm so much better than that. And I have Ryan! I don't need her anymore!*

Once the caffeine kicked in and she started feeling a little better, she took out her sketchbook and began to work on a long, bat-winged sweater with super-flared pants.

She was in the mood to start a new project in home ec. She hoped there'd be some fabric remainders in the dumpster at work that day. Printing mistakes often happened, and Trix helped herself to what she could stuff from the trash bin into her bag.

It was the one perk of toiling at Frederick Hui twenty hours a week.

Her shift started in just a few hours. She could already smell the chemicals, and they made her already weak stomach sink.

30. GIRLFRIEND

THE NEXT DAY at school Ryan was waiting. This delighted Emily. But also stabbed her with a slow shyness she didn't expect. She hopped off her heavy bike and crouched to lock it.

She squinted up at him. There were clouds, but they were wispy rather than thick and gray and they let some sun through. She stood, unfolding the full length of her body.

"So," he said, hoisting his heavy backpack further onto his shoulders. "You still my girlfriend now that we're at this dump for the week?"

Her heart trilled at the word *girlfriend*. "Okay," she said.

"Well, I don't want to talk you into anything."

"No," she said quickly. "I want to be … your girlfriend."

"Good."

"Yeah, good."

They walked into school side by side. Emily was too distracted by her new status as Ryan McElvoy's girlfriend, by their kind of coming out right there in the hallways of CHS, to think much about Trix or mourn that they hadn't met up, as usual, at the bike racks.

She noticed the school's smell, as she always did in the morning. Institutional and sweaty. Dusty. Pheromonal.

Ryan had a meeting with a rep from Gonzaga University, so he squeezed her hand and disappeared into a mass of blue and black and plaid.

Trix's desk in Johnson's class was empty. Emily slid her backpack under her feet. She could feel the burning eyes of someone, and she looked up to find April Kinsmith staring at her, along with a few others peering Emily's way.

Rachel Connelly, a ruddy-faced, wispy-haired girl, whom Emily liked well enough and who sat in front of her, twisted around and said, "You and Ryan?"

"Uh, yeah. As of Friday." She almost regretted saying the words, almost regretted that it wasn't her and Ryan's alone anymore, that they were now open to speculation and criticism.

Rachel held out her fist for a bump and said, "Good goin'."

"Thanks. I think."

From the back, April said, "So it's true."

Emily refused to acknowledge her. She opened her folder and extracted the printout of her Theatre of the Absurd assignment and set it on her desk.

"Seriously?" April snarled. "How'd you hook that up?"

Emily glanced at the door, fantasizing escape. She pretended to read her play, double-check her work.

"Jealous?" came Trix's voice. She wore her shaggy, fake-fur vest, brown leather boots that laced to the knee, and a super short denim skirt. Her hair was wild, curly as usual, but frizzy, too. Huge. And her eye makeup was twice as thick as it normally was, her lids rimmed in heavy black, with dark blue smeared to her brow bone.

"Hardly," April snapped.

"You should be," Trix said. "He's been chasing Emily for weeks. And I hear he's an amazing screw." Trix could never resist locking horns with April.

Laughter. A gasp. Emily shook her head frantically at Trix, who took her seat just as Mr. Johnson came into the room.

He called attendance. Trix pushed back her hair, belligerently flopped a notebook on her desk, and uncapped a purple pen. She didn't want to be there. But then, she didn't particularly want to be anywhere else either.

Finally, Trix met Emily's gaze and flashed a dazzling smile. "Right?" she whispered. She wanted to hurt Emily, in front of everyone. Trix wanted Emily to feel as bad as she did right then.

"I wouldn't know. And you're making a spectacle of yourself!"

"Ladies," Mr. Johnson said, looking at them pointedly.

He then instructed everyone to place their plays on the corner of his desk. He promised he'd try to get them graded by the following Monday. With scraping chairs and squishing shoe soles, they shuffled to the front of the room.

From over by the windows someone said, "Man, who farted?" A few guffaws. And then they were in their seats again.

Trix never moved. Never handed anything in.

Emily knew she should react compassionately. Her former best friend was going through something epic. Was smoking and having random sex and drinking too much and causing a ruckus wherever she went and her grades were going to plummet.

But all Emily felt for her, in that moment, was contempt. Trix couldn't even find time to do her homework? When it had been assigned weeks before? She couldn't be civil? She couldn't dress like a normal person or use a normal blue pen? She couldn't control herself at all?

31. SWEATSHOP

WHEN TRIX SAW Aaron at work the next day, he looked scared, as if she were a ghost haunting him. Good. She figured if he was scared of her, she wouldn't have to be scared of him. The jerk.

Trix stood at her station, guiding recently dyed red floral fabric around a massive paper roll. Machines did most everything there. People like Trix mostly handled quality control. It was mundane, to say the least. But it was money and, while she was at Frederick Hui, she was out of trouble.

Her mind wandered a lot while she was at work. On this particular day, spurred by the break room incident with Aaron, Trix thought about an old boyfriend of her mom's. Harold.

Harold was the worst of the string of men who'd pranced through hers and her mother's lives. At first he seemed promising, more normal than the rest. He had no piercings or tattoos. His head was full of clean-cut hair and he sported a respectable oxford shirt with khakis for his job at a check cashing joint five days a week.

"I think he's it," Trix remembered Fiona saying.

Soon, though, Harold began to betray his true self. His one vice was Bud Light, which he'd drink half a case of every night after work. Trix would watch him warily as he went to the fridge for a fresh can and tossed his empty in the kitchen sink. Over and over again.

By the sixth or seventh trip, she knew to go to her room and lock her meager door.

One night in particular, he'd gone to the refrigerator at least fourteen times (Trix could hear his footsteps and the slap of the fridge door through her walls). He'd begun arguing with her mom about what they were watching on TV. Fiona, who still smoked back then, stomped outside to have a cigarette.

There was soft tapping, and then, before she could process any of it, her door crashed inward and hung from one hinge.

Harold stood there, his chest heaving, his respectable oxford unbuttoned and the t-shirt underneath sweat stained. And then he was on top of Trix, kissing her and ripping her clothes. She tried to fight him off, but he was so much stronger than she was.

Finally, after what seemed like an hour of struggling but was probably less than five minutes, he yowled and rolled off her.

Fiona stood there with a lit cigarette in her hand like a knife. She'd just pushed it into the soft skin above his hip. In an animal voice Trix didn't recognize, her mother told Harold to leave and never come back.

Trix's hands shook as she guided the fabric through the machine. She hadn't thought about Harold in a long time. She and her mother never mentioned him or what he'd done to Trix. Which was fine with her. But occasionally, especially when she was doing something mindless, memories of him crept up.

Also, Aaron's pathetic excuse for a come on probably reminded her of what Harold had done. They were both, to varying degrees, violators.

The story of Trix's life.

She longed to take her break and have a cigarette outside (no way was she hanging out in the break room again).

Was she turning into her mother, she wondered? Would she spend her life bouncing from one loser to the next, eventually ending up on oxygen and watching bad TV while eating her weight in microwave popcorn every day?

32. Idiots Suck

IT STARTED THE next day, like she knew it eventually would. Emily and Ryan walked down the hall together between classes, sun streaming through high windows onto the tile floor, and some boy, a boy she couldn't see but could only hear, spewed, "Look, it's Olive Oil and Popeye. McElvoy, what are you doing with Stretch Lucas?"

Emily burned—her face and limbs and chest. She was already feeling ashamed because her father had found out about the Friday night party and grounded her from her camera and the computer for two weeks. And now this.

She was afraid to glance at Ryan, to see what he would do.

When neither of them responded to the idiot in the crowd, the idiot said again, "Do you have to stand on a stool to do it, McElvoy?"

Emily felt him stiffen next to her. And then he was gone, busting through the kids and chasing the idiot, who took off down the corridor and around a corner.

She was alone with her backpack and she went to American History where she opened her notebook and stared at the blank page.

She didn't see Ryan again until after school. She wanted so much not to refer to the incident that morning, but she felt like she had to. "Did you get him?" she asked.

"Nah," Ryan said, shaking his hand as if he'd punched the idiot and had sore knuckles. "What a jackass."

"Total J.A.," Emily agreed. With a sleeve, she wiped rain off her bike seat and clicked open the lock around the cross bar. Then she said, "Sorry."

"For what?"

"That it happened. It wouldn't have if you were with, you know … someone else."

Ryan closed his eyes and pretended to nod off, snoring.

She nudged him in the ribs. "You know what I mean."

"Don't be so insecure," he said.

This hurt her a little and she said, "It's not insecurity. It's reality."

"It's both." Then he asked, "Can you give me a ride on that thing? I'm wheel-less today."

"Sure." Emily gestured for him to hop on.

He held her waist, his feet hanging near the spokes.

Emily pedaled standing up. The bike was sluggish and heavy and she was conscious of her butt pumping up and down inches from his chest. When they stopped at cross streets, she noticed his fingers, which had found their way under her vest and sweater to her skin. They pressed firmly, hotly. She imagined, later, finding ten red ellipses where the pads of his fingers had rested along her rib cage.

Ryan directed her to his house, a gray-blue cedar shake bungalow with white trim. It was small, but tidy. A UW flag acted as a curtain for an upstairs window. On the porch sat an old box fan, its cord wound neatly, and a rake, a few leaves stuck in its tines.

It didn't look like anyone was home, but Ryan didn't invite her in.

"See you tomorrow then," she said.

He leaned in to kiss her and his forehead knocked her helmet's brim. He turned his head and tried again. "In the a.m.," he said.

She didn't wait for him to unlock the door. She took off, her heart leaden. Was he mad at her? Did that incident at school change how he felt?

It started to rain. "Perfect," she said.

As her tires sluiced through mud puddles and soggy leaves, she couldn't shake the thought that finding her mother and establishing some sort of relationship with her would make this tallness of hers more bearable. That understanding where she came from and watching another woman her height move through the world with some sort of grace would give her hope. It seemed to be the key to accepting this huge body and all the disappointments that came along with it.

When Emily got home, water dripped from her hair and glued her clothes to her skin.

She peeled off the wet stuff and stepped right into a hot shower. She had to duck under the showerhead, something she rarely noticed but today seemed an affront.

She whacked the cold tile wall with her hand. It stung. The sting was good. She whacked it again, harder. Again and again. Until she was on her knees in the tub, pounding the porcelain.

A knock came on the door. Then Melissa's voice. "Em? Kristen? What's going on in there? You okay?"

"Yes!" Emily called. She knew Melissa meant well, but she didn't want her. Melissa didn't get it. At all. "Go away!"

No more knocks came and she assumed Melissa had uncharacteristically retreated. But when Emily swiped the shower curtain back and reached for a towel, she saw her sitting there on the closed toilet, her arms crossed over her chest. Emily bellowed, "God! Get out!"

"You seem upset," Melissa said, her voice infuriatingly calm.

Back behind the curtain, Emily buried her face in a thick, burgundy towel, shaking her head. Melissa was too much.

"Wanna talk?"

"If I wanted to talk would I have told you to go? Now, please, leave." Emily started to cry. She tried to muffle her sobs with the towel, but knew Melissa heard.

"Honey, I just want to help."

"Don't call me honey. And you can't help." She wiped her snotty nose on the terry cloth. She heard the exhaust fan come on.

After what seemed like a half hour, Melissa said, "Okay. Will you come to me if you need anything?"

To appease her, Emily said, "Yeah, fine. I will."

And Melissa, thankfully, in a sweep of cool air, left, the door clicking behind her.

Emily dried herself and dressed quickly, not trusting that Melissa wouldn't come back, reading aloud from a parenting manual about how teenagers need constant convincing to communicate, about how the adult must keep trying, or lose all influence with said teenager.

If she weren't banned from the computer, Emily would've found some article emailed to her about girls and self esteem. Melissa liked to do that. Text little tidbits of "wisdom," email stories she thought were relevant, but were actually only relevant if you were thirty or forty and thought you were getting an inside track into the brain of your sixteen-year-old.

33. THE HIGH LIFE

THE EGG CAME nested in one of those little cups you only saw people eating out of on TV or in the children's book *Bread and Jam for Frances*. "How cutesy," Trix said to Marjorie as she cracked it and began the arduous peeling. She sprinkled it with lots of salt and ate hungrily. She should make eggs at home. It would be an easy dinner.

Marjorie chowed down on a head-sized chocolate chip cookie, doing an espresso shot after every few bites. She had five tiny cups lined up in front of her and went down the row, slamming them back.

Even for Trix, Marjorie's caffeine consumption was too intense. Give Trix a strong Americano and she was good. That many espresso shots and she'd be bouncing off the walls.

A few minutes earlier, she'd seen Emily pass the window, pedaling her bike with Ryan on the seat. She and Marjorie had laughed uproariously, but Trix actually felt her stomach sink to her toes. And then the ants came marching up her arms and legs.

"What's wrong with you?" Marjorie had barked.

"Allergies," Trix said as she scratched.

"Isn't there a pill for that?"

"I forget to take them," she said. She didn't explain she was allergic to envy. And that she freaking hated herself for it.

Marjorie downed her third shot. "I'm feelin' the buzz!"

Trix stuffed half the egg in her mouth, then cupped the round, white over her tongue and stuck it out at her friend.

Marjorie laughed and took another shot. "What do you wanna do tonight?" Marjorie didn't believe in homework. Her grades showed it, too. She wasn't planning on college and said all she needed after high school was to earn enough to pay for a room in a house on Capitol Hill, cookies, coffee, and "substances."

"I think I need to do some sketching."

"Need?"

"Yeah. If I go too long without it I start to get the DTs. Kind of spazzy. It helps."

"Really? Sketching?"

"My designs. It's a hobby." It didn't seem like she could confide in Marjorie her future plans yet. Ambition wasn't something Marjorie understood.

"Ah, high on life," Marjorie said sarcastically.

"Sort of."

That was at least something Emily understood about Trix. They both had artistic visions and would sometimes hang out for hours, Emily taking and editing photos, and Trix scheming fantastical clothes and putting them down on paper.

She pushed the thought of Emily from her mind. Shared artistic vision didn't make up for everything else.

"Oh c'mon," Marjorie said, drinking her fourth shot. "Go out with us. We'll fill your tank."

Trix knew taking her sketchbook to the park or a café would be good for her. But at the same time, she liked that Marjorie wanted her to be part of her group. The thought of what trouble they might stir up excited her, made her feel alive.

She looked up at the exposed ductwork on the ceiling. "Okay," she said. She'd let herself, for another night, be swept into Marjorie's brume of crazy.

34. ATTENTION, UNWANTED

EMILY SMELLED THE mango hair product and fresh nail polish before she looked up and noticed April lurking next to her locker. At first she thought April was waiting for another girl, Liz, whom April sometimes hung with and whose locker was a few down from Emily's. But then she noticed April staring at her, her eyes loud and blue.

"You know that Ryan McElvoy used to go out with Jessie Turner, right?" April said.

Emily scowled. She did remember Ryan was linked to Jessie the summer before, but tried not to think about it much. "And your point would be … ?"

"My point is," April said, adjusting the bangles on her arm. "Jessie dumped him. He still wants her, so I've heard. Just a friendly heads up."

Swapping out the books in her backpack, Emily slammed her locker closed and wished Trix were standing right there, slinging her clever, cruel words back at April. Emily said, "Okay. Thanks for that. You're selfless, April, really. Always looking out for others."

"No worries," April said, pivoted, and walked away, tiny butt and long hair swaying.

Emily was pretty sure she hated April.

She was also pretty sure Trix was insane. That afternoon, Trix wasn't in English Comp and the buzz was that she and Marjorie were suspended because, the day before, they'd started their own little rainbow party in a second floor boys' bathroom.

Emily pictured the road Trix was headed down and, instead of an interesting old brick lane that went through charming towns, past fantastic architecture, and led to her own design label, it now resembled skinny, dark alleys lined with smelly dumpsters and puddles of pee.

Emily wasn't able to think about it for long though, because Mr. Johnson called on her.

Crap. "Yes?"

"Your play."

"Yes."

"I'd like you to come up and read it, please. Aloud to the class."

As Emily made her way to the front of the room, her heart thumping hard, everyone's eyes on her, including Ryan's, Mr. Johnson said, "Folks. Ms. Lucas's was the best interpretation of this assignment I read. That I've read from any student. And I've taught for fourteen years. It encompassed all the elements I asked for and incorporated them with a flare that, frankly, I didn't know high school juniors possessed. No offense to the rest of you."

Please stop, Emily thought.

When she reached him, he handed her the stapled pages and said, "Nicely done. If I gave out A-plusses, this would've earned one."

Emily's voice, when she first started reading, sounded okay. Smooth and amplified. But soon, as she stood there realizing everyone was watching and listening and wondering what on earth had garnered such praise from Johnson, her larynx began to vibrate.

She tried not to hear whispering. A snicker. Tried not to think about Trix out in the city somewhere, leaving blue lipstick marks on cigarettes and … other things. Tried not to wonder if Ryan was wishing he were still with Jessie Turner.

There was a small part of Emily that was proud of her play, yes. She'd worked hard on it and liked that Johnson recognized this. It made her feel smart. But mostly she wanted to not be in front of the class, in that moment, giving their judgmental souls her words.

By the time she finished, her breath was coming in long puffs and sweat dotted her upper lip. She took her seat, fanning herself with her paper.

"Can anyone tell me what was so astonishing about Ms. Lucas's work?" Mr. Johnson asked.

Shut. Up.

No one raised his or her hand or spoke up.

"Two girls are waiting for the phone to ring. Presumably for a boy to call. Their conversation, typical of a conversation between teenagers, goes nowhere," Johnson says. A few kids chuckle. "Yet you can see them trying to figure out their place in the world, in the universe, just by reading this round and round dialogue. Good work, Ms. Lucas," he said.

"Thank you," Emily mumbled, relieved to be back behind her desk.

She slouched down in her seat and stuffed the paper into her notebook. It wasn't that she was ungrateful to have gotten a good grade. She just wasn't in the mood to have been singled out.

She was never in the mood to be singled out.

35. A DISAPPOINTMENT TO EVERYONE

FIONA'S STUBBY FINGERS were greasy from fake popcorn butter. She wiped them on a paper towel and rubbed her forehead. "What am I gonna do with you?" she wailed.

Trix sat on the one living room chair. Rodney wasn't there, for once. He was out applying for a job at a tire shop. "Nothing," Trix said. "As usual."

Her mother looked at Trix from under her still-shiny hand. "Oh, so that's what this was about? You're trying to get my attention?"

Trix wrapped a coppery curl around her pinky. She considered this. Had she done it to get her mother's attention? Her father's? Emily's?

She didn't think so. She'd just gotten carried away with Marjorie.

"And in the school bathroom?" her mother hissed. "Good God, Trixie. What were you thinking?"

That was the point. She hadn't been thinking. She'd been living and feeling. She shrugged. And then she did something unthinkable. She pulled out her pack of cigarettes and lit one up right in front of Fiona.

Mouth hanging open, her mother stood and sputtered. "You put that out right now. What's wrong with you? That could kill me! And you. You know what those things have done to my lungs."

Trix just looked at her mom and took a drag.

"You put that out or you put yourself out. You hear me? I will not have a smoker living under this roof!"

Standing, cigarette hanging from between her lips, Trix went into her bedroom and threw some clothes, makeup, and her sketchbook into a small suitcase she owned but never used. She grabbed David's cardboard box and some dry food. He was outside, so she went to find him.

Her mother stuck her head out the door. "Where are you going?"

Around her cigarette, Trix yelled back, "I don't know yet." She called for David, shook his food around in the box so he'd hear it.

"Don't get more mixed up with that awful girl who got you into this trouble."

"How do you know it wasn't me who got *her* into trouble?"

Her mom began to cry then. "Put out that cigarette and get back in here."

But it was too late. Trix realized she couldn't stay, couldn't watch her mother continue to go through men like tissues. She didn't want to live in a trailer on Aurora anymore. She didn't especially want to be the girl who hosted a rainbow party in the school bathroom either. But that sort of life seemed to be her destiny for now.

She did squash the cigarette butt out under her boot. "I can't," she said.

Trix saw David then, sitting on the corner of someone else's stoop and licking his front paw. She strode over and scooped him up. He purred as she stuffed him into his box.

She walked away to the sound of her mom weeping, the rush of traffic, and the mews of David, wondering where they were going.

About a half mile down Aurora, after enduring catcalls and honks, she sidelined into the parking lot of a carpet remnant store and opened her crappy cell phone to call her dad. Her phone battery, though, was dead. Damn!

Shoving the phone back into her pocket, she continued to the nearest bus stop and waited. She poked her fingers into David's box and tried to comfort him.

She got on the first bus that showed up and calculated how to get down to Beacon Hill where her dad lived. It would take two transfers. Fine. She had nothing but time.

Earbuds in, cat box on her lap, and mind numbed, she rode through the early evening hoping that when she got to her dad's place he wouldn't turn her away.

36. NONPARENT NUMBER 2

HE LIVED ON one side of a ramshackle duplex. Where a lawn should be was a smudge of dirt and a sagging, three-legged carport covered his truck. Trix had been there a few times before. It always smelled like pot and mildew.

She knocked three times, worried that even though his truck was there, he wouldn't be (he was known to catch rides from friends to all corners of the state) or that he'd be passed out on the couch. Finally, though, the door swung inward and her dad stood there wearing jeans with no shirt, his hair twist-tied back, as usual.

"Huh?" he said, clearly out of it.

"I need to stay here for a few days," Trix said.

"Whaddya mean a few days?"

She pushed past him, set her stuff down, and opened the windows. "Mom kicked me out." This was an exaggeration, she knew. But she needed her dad's sympathy so he'd let her stay. "God almighty it reeks in here."

He let the door close and followed her in. Clumsily, he pushed a stack of papers off a torn, plaid couch and offered her a place to sit.

Still standing, she crossed her arms over her chest. David meowed, wanting out of his box. She freed him and her dad chortled. "That damn cat again?"

"He's sweet. And he does all his business outside, remember? He's no trouble at all. Swear."

Her dad shook his head and buried his face in his hands like he couldn't believe his bad luck to be saddled with his teenage daughter and her fleabag pet. "Why'd your mother kick you out?" His words were slurred and his eyes glassy. She hated seeing him like this. He looked like a moron, trying to pretend he was some stoner kid, when really he was just a pathetic middle-aged man who'd never grown up.

"You really want to know?" Trix asked. She felt her determination leave, replaced by deep exhaustion. She scooped up David and sat on the cracked coffee table, sighing. "I got suspended from school."

"For what?" Her dad took her spot on the couch.

"For being slutty."

This made him cackle. "What do they care what you do off school grounds?"

"It was on school grounds."

He looked at her, his eyes seeming to clear some.

"I know," she said. "I know. Okay?" She couldn't come right out and say how contrite she was or how cheap she felt. She had to keep the badass wall up. Because otherwise ... well, she couldn't think about what would happen otherwise.

Leaning forward and pointing at her, he said, "Don't you go gettin' yourself knocked up, ruin your whole life."

She wasn't about to let that happen and she told him so.

He glowered as if he didn't believe her. "Like mother, like daughter," he said.

"No!" Trix barked. But beneath her rebellious facade, she knew. She could end up just like Fiona. Sure, maybe Fiona's clothes hadn't been as cool and maybe her artistic talent had gone neglected after having kids, but deep down, weren't Trix and her mother more alike than Trix wanted to admit? "I will not be her. Ever."

"Then you need to get yourself on a different track, girly," her dad said.

He went into the kitchen, grabbed two beers out of the fridge, and handed her one. He lay down on the couch and turned his head sideways to take long draws from his bottle. He belched, and repeated, "You need to get yourself on a different track." Then he closed his eyes.

"I'm trying Dad. I'm working and saving, okay?"

"Saving for what? Whiskey sours at the Buckaroo?" he slurred.

"A sewing machine. So I can make my designs and get them out there. Designing clothes is all I've ever wanted and I thought you knew that!"

Her dad grunted, then began to snore.

Trix chewed her lips in frustration. She threw a ratty afghan over him, turned the TV on low and sat with David, watching until she, too, fell asleep.

37. FRIENDSHIP MASHUP

EMILY HAD BEEN reduced to rolling her jeans so it looked like she actually wanted them short. One day in early November, she folded up the hems a couple times, threw on a charcoal gray sweater and red scarf and waved shyly at Ryan when she saw him in school.

"Hey Bean," he said, distracted by a broken zipper on his backpack.

"Hey." She remembered a day she'd come into school when he'd pushed a strand of hair behind her ear and said, "You," as he gazed into her eyes.

This was nothing like that. He seemed different. Flustered. His eyes were red and dull. Stubble dotted his jaw. A big coffee stain was splattered across one sleeve.

He glanced down the corridor, then looked sheepish. "I have to finish a report before first period starts."

"No sweat," she said. "Lunch?"

"Aw, wish I could. I have to make up lab time in McD's." Which was shorthand for Mr. McDouglas, a chemistry teacher everyone loved because of his tough yet fair way of instructing. "Maybe we can study tonight."

"Okay," she said too quickly.

"I just have to check something first though. Let me get back to you."

She watched him turn and move away.

Just then, Trix's new friend Marjorie sidled up and said, "You should pick on someone your own height."

Emily died a little inside as Ryan caught the criticism, turned and stopped. She waved him away and pivoted so her back was to him.

Trix was nowhere to be found. If she had been there and siding with Emily, she would've come up with something like, "You should pick on someone with your own IQ." But Trix was not there and definitely not on Emily's side.

"I thought you were suspended," Emily said.

Marjorie lowered her voice and her eyelids and murmured, "That was last week. Freak."

Emily couldn't contain her anger. "You're the one with the black lipstick and bullring in your nose, and I'm the freak?"

Marjorie slowly raised her foot behind her, then kicked a nearby locker with her platform boot. The chaos in the hallway rendered her kick soundless, but still, Emily jumped.

After Marjorie sauntered away, Emily escaped to the bathroom and flattened herself against the tile wall's heater vent.

She thought she was blessedly alone, until she heard a voice ask, "Getting warm?" It was Kennedy, the third Farkette, applying lip gloss and looking at Emily in the mirror.

Emily silently groaned. She did not need a run-in with one of them. Not then. She said, "I guess."

Kennedy tossed her gloss into a pocket of her tote bag. She came over and stood right in front of Emily "Hey," she said. "I'm sorry about April and Vanessa. The way they treat you and Trix. I'm not a part of that. Just FYI."

Right. Emily didn't trust Kennedy. Kennedy was trying to lure her in by creating a false sense of security. She'd be nice to Emily, get her to let her guard down, and then the Farkettes would pounce in some sort of humiliating way. They'd tackle her and write Jolly Green Giant across her forehead in lipstick or take and circulate video of Emily in the locker room.

"Okayyy," Emily said warily. Wanting Kennedy to leave, she rifled through her backpack to make herself look busy.

But Kennedy had decided to hang around, seemed ready to talk more. "So, you and Ryan McElvoy, huh?"

Kennedy was gorgeous with long black hair and faintly Filipino features. Today she wore tights, tall boots, and a baggy dress. She stood with her hands in her pockets.

"Yes," Emily said. Why did everyone find that so hard to believe? But then, she sometimes found it hard to believe, to relax into it and enjoy the ride. Especially the last few days when it had become clear that something was super off with him.

"Hmm."

The bell rang, an echoey trill that never failed to launch Emily right out of her skin.

"So obnoxious," Kennedy muttered. Then, to Emily, "So you'll remember what I said, right? I am not April or Vanessa."

Emily couldn't stop what slithered from her mouth next, like a long snake impossible to gulp down. "Why are you friends with them?"

Kennedy shrugged. "Because they're nice when you get to know them. Which is to say, they're just as insecure and lonely as the rest of us. They just don't hide it as well." She then gathered her tote bag, slung it over her shoulders and, with a small wave, left the bathroom.

Lagging a few minutes behind, Emily thought about what Kennedy had said. April and Vanessa seemed the least insecure, lonely people she could imagine. But then, from all the anti-bullying assemblies the school loved to hold, she knew that insecurity was what usually drove meanness. Hence, Trix's recent crappy treatment of her.

Emily went about the rest of her day, trying not to think of Marjorie and their little confrontation first thing that morning.

After school she glimpsed Trix. She was crossing 15th, smoking, and talking animatedly with Marjorie. They stepped up onto the curb in tandem and laughed about something.

Emily's chest clenched. And she knew her heart was just an organ, just a pumping muscle, but it felt, truly felt, like it had squeezed into a hard, hurting fist.

38. WEARY

TRIX WAS TIRED of Emily's wounded gaze, like she was trying to look inside her, to figure her out. Trix didn't know what the big mystery was. All Emily had to do was turn her scrutiny toward her annoyingly sane life, maybe listen to how she talked to Trix as if she were some loser always making the wrong choices.

Trix left school that Friday without bothering to get books from her locker. She went out into the overcast afternoon where she scanned the throngs for Marjorie.

It was Emily who came through the doors, though, without her boy toy for once. "Hey," she said to Trix. "I've been looking for you."

"Oh yeah?" Trix tapped ash off the end of her cigarette and tried not to meet Emily's eyes.

"Can we talk?"

"I don't see the point."

"You don't see the point?" Emily hoisted her backpack further up her shoulder. "We're best friends, or we were, and we're not even speaking. I miss you, Trix."

I miss you too, Trix thought. Then chastised herself. What was there to miss? They had nothing in common anymore. *Keep the wall up. Keep the wall up.* But even as she chanted this over and over in her head, a lump the size of a robin's egg rose in her throat. She had to get rid of Emily or she was going to cry. And if she started crying, she didn't know that she could stop. Besides, Marjorie would be out any minute.

"I don't have anything to say to you," she said, making her eyes white hot lasers of cruelty. "Okay? Nothing. Now leave me alone."

Emily stepped back as if she'd been slapped. "I feel like I don't know you anymore."

"Exactly."

Just then Marjorie burst forth with Isaac and her gang of hoodlums. She gave Emily a hearty sneer, which Trix thought was a little much, then pulled Trix away.

"We're going to shoot BBs at fishing boats," she crowed.

As Trix was dragged down the sidewalk, she took one last look at Emily, who stood hunched with Ryan now. He rubbed her back and said something into her ear.

The ants started in behind Trix's knees this time, skittering relentlessly over her calves and around her heels. The tickle of their dainty feet was excruciating.

She'd get drunk that night, she decided. So drunk and numb she wouldn't be able to feel the tiny bodies traipsing across her skin. "Do you have anything?" she asked Marjorie. Shorthand, of course, for anything illegal, anything fun.

Marjorie sucked hard on her cigarette. "Don't I always?"

39. The Stepmom Conundrum

EMILY COULDN'T STOP thinking about emailing her mom. Her real mom who lived as an artist in Bisbee, Arizona with a possible new husband.

She typed several drafts of what she wanted to say, deleting it all and starting again. She fretted. What if her mom never responded? What if she told Emily she had no interest and to please leave her alone? Or worse, what if she wrote back, *Who are you*?

Frustrated, she wandered down to the family room. She watched a celebrity gossip show while Melissa played with a new pedometer she'd just gotten online. Melissa walked around the room, looked at the digital display, took several more steps, did a few lunges, then punched buttons.

Just after a story about Michelle Williams and Matilda, Emily hit mute on the remote and said, "Is it, like, totally odd being a stepmom?"

Melissa stopped, looked up from her new toy and said, "What? You're asking me a question? About myself and my feelings?"

"I am."

"Wow."

"Yeah. So, is it?"

"Totally weird? I don't know. In the beginning it was an adjustment for sure. But one I was willing to make because I love your dad. And, of course, I've come to love you and Kristen."

Emily felt she was expected to tell Melissa she loved her back, but the words caught in her throat like a gristled hunk of beef. Did she? Love Melissa? She'd always seen her as sort of an interloper. A makeshift replacement for a real mom. Love had never seemed to enter the equation. At least not for Emily.

Melissa continued, "I mean, your dad and I have been married ten years now. I've gotten used to my role here, I think."

Emily nodded and ran her finger up and down an outside seam of her old jeans. "Did you ever want kids of your own?" she asked.

At that, Melissa's eyes flitted away and she resumed tapping at her pedometer. "Well, yeah," she said. "Sometimes."

"How many would you have wanted?"

"Two. A boy and a girl," she said so quickly that it was obvious she often thought about children of her own.

"But my dad doesn't want more."

"I think … he's too wounded … by what your mom did. He'll never trust me enough to have a child with me."

Emily said, "But he married you!"

"It's not the same," Melissa insisted. She headed toward the kitchen. "I need a snack. Do you want some yogurt sprinkled with flax seeds and wheat germ?" She waggled her eyebrows, knowing her offer was not at all tempting to Emily.

"I'd rather have a cream puff."

"On your own time," Melissa said, and was gone.

The TV still blared. Emily half watched it. Half thought about what Melissa said. About what she'd given up to marry Emily's grumpy, old dad. She wondered what Melissa saw in him, what mysterious quality he possessed that persuaded her to give up her dream of kids. Because there was no way having two step-daughters—ungrateful little kids who grew into surly teenagers—could replace making your own babies.

Emily thought about her mother again and how she'd had what Melissa wanted, but had thrown it all away.

40. Gym Hell

FARK'S KNEES RESTED on her elbows, butt pointing toward the ceiling. Her face red, she said, "This is a tripod, people." Then, defying gravity, she straightened her legs until she was doing a full on headstand. She stayed that way for a minute or two, long enough for her shirt to slip down toward her chin, exposing half moons of her no-nonsense beige bra.

When she flipped back upright, the blood drained from her face and she yelled, "Everyone take a spot along the wall."

The guys and girls were in PE together that day, though, Ryan, thankfully, didn't take this particular class.

Still, the entire perimeter of the gym was filled with juniors, and each person got about eight inches of space along the concrete block wall.

Emily began to sweat. She couldn't do this. She didn't know how to move her long body that way.

"Okay, everyone on their knees!" Fark said and chuckled. "Now, head down on the floor, do the tripod."

So everyone did. Everyone, that was, except Emily and a handful of obese kids like Brenna Toast and Andrew Colmilker, who didn't even pretend to try, but just sat, picking at their fingernails. Fark usually ignored them, figuring they were too far-gone to be worth her trouble.

But she noticed Emily struggling, like a daddy longlegs that'd been flipped on its back. Her limbs wouldn't cooperate. Everyone, every upside down person in the room, could see Emily flailing.

Trix was there somewhere, along the west wall. Doing what Fark said for once.

Fark walked toward Emily, her sneakers soundless over the polished wood floor. "Your center of balance is too high," she sniped.

Standing, Emily glared at her. *No shit, Sherlock,* she wanted to say. Instead she focused on breathing. What did Fark expect Emily to do about her too-high center of balance?

The gym was quiet, everyone on their heads.

"You need to get your butt up in the air," Fark commanded. "Try again."

But Emily knew she couldn't, knew she wouldn't bend herself into that vulnerable position with Fark looming over her, snapping instructions.

"I can't," she said.

"Then you may as well go get dressed," Fark spit.

"Fine." Emily strode across the gym and down the rubber-lined stairs. She changed in the locker room and wandered the quiet hallways, finding her way to a side door and darting out into the cloudy afternoon. It was only one thirty and darkness already loomed.

Walking south on 15th, Emily hopped a bus going downtown. It was good to be there, smashed against the window, warm, the burr of the engine calming her.

She got off in Belltown and walked to Shutter Joe, early for her shift but doubting Thomas would mind.

Putting on her apron and signing her time card, she set about the task of washing stainless steel pitchers and coffee cups. "The glamorous life of a Seattle barista," Thomas said as he passed with a tub full of more dirty dishes.

"It's nothing compared to what I just came from," she said, then elaborated on the awfulness of being one of the only kids unable to stand on her head.

"Oh, because you'll need that skill for future job interviews," he said.

She laughed, but her mood was dark. She wanted things that bothered her to not. Fark, Trix, who was fading from her life like an apparition, Ryan and his offness, and Marilyn Wozniak.

None of it should matter so much.

But all of it did.

41. INKED

FOR TRIX, LIVING with her dad wasn't so different from living with her mom, except that, if possible, she had less accountability than she did before. Like Fiona, her dad didn't ask about homework or give her a curfew or make sure she ate vegetables. He occasionally cooked them both potpies or held out a shaky hand to offer her a five-dollar bill. But that was as far as his fatherly instincts took him.

At least there was no Rodney. No string of failed relationships to witness. And Trix could smoke at will. Her dad didn't care and, in fact, sometimes smoked with her. She'd talked him into watching less TV and had even brought him some historical books from the library, a genre she remembered him liking once upon a time. On a couple instances, she caught him reading, a can of beer nestled between his thighs. And she felt like she was making the tiniest positive difference in his life.

Trix had stopped seeing Marjorie as an impossibly cool, almost untouchable figure and started noticing her small insecurities, like how she kept her legs covered at all times, in baggy jeans or long black skirts, and the way she only smiled with her mouth closed, to hide her crooked teeth. Also there was her extreme avoidance of discussion about her family. After that first day at Golden Gardens when they'd compared moms, if you even mentioned the word *parent* she jammed her fingers in her ears and sang, "They don't matter. They don't matter."

Still, even with Marjorie's self doubt revealed, Trix wanted her approval.

Trix and Marjorie were together at Trix's dad's one Sunday afternoon. Trix was tired from her shift at Frederick Hui, guzzling a Diet Coke, and washing her face with steaming hot water and soap. Marjorie flipped through her phone and suddenly said, "I need more ink! A skull right here." She came into the bathroom and pointed at a spot behind her left ear. She already had a homemade tattoo of a hand grenade on her right wrist and something scrolly along her lower back.

"Okay," Trix shrugged.

"Remember that Magpie guy? We met him down at Isaac's?"

"Not really."

"He's a tattoo artist. He said he'd give me whatever I want. I just have to call before I come in."

"For free?"

"Yeah! Duh. I have zero cash."

Resentment flared in Trix. It was like it didn't even occur to Marjorie to get a job, to earn some of her own money instead of mooching off guys she met at parties. She asked, "What's he going to expect in return?"

Marjorie rolled her eyes and left the bathroom.

When Trix had cleaned up and felt somewhat human again, she and Marjorie scrounged around the fridge for food, came up with a jar of peanut butter, hot dog buns, and a squeeze bottle of jam. "Oh, Dad," she muttered, shaking her head. She supposed she'd have to buy groceries for him, too.

They made PBJs on buns, wolfed them down while standing in the kitchen, then left the sad, foodless duplex.

Trix and Marjorie took the bus up to Shoreline, where Isaac's tattoo artist friend worked. They looked through big binders of designs. One woman was in a corner chair getting something inked around her upper arm. Trix wondered how much it hurt.

Isaac's friend, Magpie, worked on someone else but said he'd have an opening in about half an hour.

Trix felt very Emily-ish as she said, "Do you want to think about it for a while? Maybe come back another day?"

"No!" Marjorie boomed. "I know what I want and where I want it."

"Okay. Good."

"What are you getting?" Marjorie asked.

Trix hadn't planned on any tattoos that day. Not that she was opposed to it. In fact, a tattoo was something she aspired to; she just hadn't ever set the wheels in motion to actually get one. "Should I?" she said, suddenly excited. She'd pay cash for it, though.

"Hell to the yeah!"

She flipped through the binders with renewed interest. She wanted to get a tattoo that meant something. Maybe some writing. But what?

In the end, she decided on an abstract, Picassoesque profile of a woman's face. Her expression was strong and sad and purposeful. Trix thought it looked like a tattoo a fashion designer would have.

As Marjorie discussed her skull with Magpie, Trix saw an unmistakable leer in his eyes and hoped he wasn't expecting what she thought he might be expecting for his services. Trix asked, "How much is this going to cost?"

Marjorie shot Trix the stink eye for reminding Magpie that money was generally exchanged for tattoos. "I just think we should have all the information," Trix said accusingly, crossing her arms.

Magpie scratched his patchy beard. He was skinny and unhealthy looking, like someone who ate PBJ on hot dog buns for every meal. If he even ate.

"I take trade," he said and began stenciling the outline of the skull on Marjorie's neck.

Trix looked at Marjorie, knowing panic was in her own eyes. Marjorie, though, shrugged and said, "That's what I was hoping."

Okay, fine. Marjorie was her own person. If she wanted to give this guy a blowjob or whatever so she could get a free tattoo, who was Trix to judge her? And, after what she and Marjorie had done with those guys in the school bathroom a few weeks before, Trix knew she shouldn't talk. But she realized, as she stood there in Shoreline Ink, that she did not want to prostitute herself for services. For attention was one thing, but what Marjorie was doing was another rung up the whorishness ladder.

Maybe it was ridiculous of her to differentiate the two. But she did.

She went to the bank of windows facing 175th. Loud music crashed through the place, and, between songs, the tinny buzz of needles echoed. She was having second thoughts about getting her own tattoo here. Did she really want Magpie touching her?

After a while, Trix went back to Marjorie, who sat on a bench with her head ratcheted to the side. Magpie wore black rubber gloves, a huge serpent tattoo wrapping around his throat and up the side of his mostly hairless scalp.

Marjorie cringed a little, but Trix couldn't tell if it was because of the needle pulsating in and out of her, or because of the unnatural position of her head.

Fifteen minutes later, it was done. A small black skull, surrounded by angry red skin, grimaced from Marjorie's neck.

"We'll settle up later," Magpie said. "You gonna be at Isaac's tomorrow night?"

"I can be."

"Awright, see you there, then."

He turned to Trix and said, "I have nothing but time. You want one?"

"Nah."

"C'mon. You look like a chick who should have some tats."

Trix did have her heart set on the woman's profile now.

She shrugged.

"Jesus! Just sit down on the bench and do it!" Marjorie commanded.

Trix sighed. She detested being bullied into things. She really did want the tattoo, though. "Okay, but I'm paying cash."

"Suit yourself," Magpie said.

"That's so stupid," Marjorie said, gingerly touching her neck. "You could get it for free."

Trix laid down on the padded bench and gave Magpie her forearm. She said, "Nothing's free." If she'd learned one thing in her life, she'd learned that.

42. WARNING

IT WAS ON Friday morning, when Emily, tired from the week, trudged to a pep assembly she had no desire to attend. Kennedy Furukawa sidled up to her, looking adorable as usual in a denim miniskirt, black leather boots and a fuzzy turquoise sweater. "Hey," she said.

"Hey," Emily replied. She was still suspicious of Kennedy, despite her niceness in the bathroom a few weeks before.

"Watch your back," Kennedy said.

Emily nerdily turned around. "What do you mean?"

"Straight ahead," Kennedy said. "Here I'm going to hand you a paper so it looks like we're exchanging class notes." She passed Emily a lined sheet that said, *Someone wants your boyfriend.*

Emily kept her face stony, but her heart plummeted to her toes. "Who?" she hissed.

Kennedy cocked a brow and veered away like a sleek Lamborghini exiting a freeway.

The gym was packed on both sides with kids. Hand painted banners hung along the walls that said, "Let's go, Wolves!" "Wolves #1!" and "Show them how it's done!" There was the peculiar drone and collective murmur of so many people contributing to separate conversations at once.

Emily scanned the crowd for someone she knew. Trix wouldn't be there. She'd never in a million years attend a pep rally. She was probably out smoking with Marjorie, or worse, with a guy somewhere.

Ryan sat with some of his friends up toward the top, against the far wall. She could see him talking on his cell phone and, because of what Kennedy had just told her, wondered who was on the other end of the call.

She took an open spot and fiddled with her own phone so she wouldn't have to talk. She was still absorbing what Kennedy had told her. Emily wasn't surprised someone wanted her boyfriend. Lots of someones surely wanted him. He was wonderful and cute and smart and funny.

But the way Kennedy had told her to watch her back make it clear that an attempt on his heart was in the works.

It didn't mean the attempt would be successful, Emily reminded herself. Ryan had a brain of his own and he'd been the one to pursue her, after all.

She wondered if he still liked her as much as he had in the beginning. If her habit of cracking her knuckles or *growing several inches a month* was bugging him.

To put the issue out of her mind, she texted Kristen. *U Here?*
By north hoop.

Emily looked up and, faintly, saw her sister. She gave her a peace sign.

The thundering began, a bunch of overly spirited kids stomping their feet, one-two-one, one-two-one, to bring out the basketball players.

Soon they appeared, the team in white, gold, and green uniforms. Their sneakers squeaked across the highly polished court. They took turns shooting, reaping wild cheers when they made baskets and disappointed *Ooohs* when they missed.

The marching band played, its brass and percussion echoing through the hot gym.

Mr. Astley, the athletic director, introduced the players and their positions, and got the crowd screaming until their faces were red. At which point Emily tuned out and thought about her mom and Winslow, imagined them at that very moment down in Arizona, sitting on their patio and watching lizards dart in and out of cactus. Cacti? Would they be drinking iced tea or lemonade or cocktails? Emily had no idea. Would her mother wear shorts or a long flowing skirt? Did she prefer her hair back off her neck, or down? Did she and Winslow get along, or would they be arguing about landscaping, about their broken sink faucet, about the cost of things, like Emily's dad and Melissa often did?

She wondered if she'd ever learn the answers, or if she'd spend the rest of her life speculating.

13. RAVE

DESPITE HOW SKEEVY Magpie was, and that Marjorie reportedly disappeared with him into a bedroom at Isaac's the day after Marjorie and Trix had gotten their tattoos, Trix loved the woman's profile on her arm. She rubbed the special salve into it, and the sunburned feeling was subsiding.

She began wearing short sleeves every day so she could show it off. And when her dad saw it, he grunted, "Huh. Cool," and, drinking copious amounts of beer, carried on reading about Teddy Roosevelt on the Amazon River.

The tattoo seemed to be a concrete measure of her badassedness, something that said, *I'm tough and nothing I do affects me very much.* If she stared at it long enough, she actually began to believe the words.

One Saturday night in mid-December, Marjorie suggested they go to a rave in SODO. Trix jumped at the chance to put on a tank top and dance around with other sweaty bodies. Her tattoo would be out there for all to see. Besides, she hadn't been to a rave yet and wanted to check one out.

It was in a dark warehouse where everyone received two glow sticks as they entered. On a slightly elevated stage, a DJ wearing a black t-shirt that said Kryptonite in fluorescent letters spun frenetic electronica, kind of reminding Trix of Emily's favorite music.

A light show played on the ceiling above them. A bunch of people danced. Others stood around drinking Red Bulls and Mountain Dew.

After roaming the perimeter of the party for a while, Marjorie said, "I need something to loosen me up."

There was no bar, but Trix did see a woman in a vinyl jester outfit walking around like a cigarette girl, passing out small paper squares. Acid, she guessed.

"How much?" Marjorie yelled over the music.

"Ten bucks, but there's two hits per blotter!"

Marjorie batted her lashes at Isaac and he handed over a ten-dollar bill. They ripped the square in half and each put a piece on their tongues. "You gonna buy one?" she asked Trix.

Trix shrugged. She was tempted. But ten dollars could also buy three or four boxes of cereal, a pound of good coffee that would last for weeks, or part of a sweet sewing machine. Besides, she'd already spent fifty bucks on the tattoo. And no, she wasn't going to ask a guy for the money.

She decided to just start dancing and see what happened.

There was an old jalopy in the middle of the warehouse that people stood on and undulated around. It was fun. Trix felt like the beat was pounding from inside her, out. And she was able to forget her responsibilities and missteps for a while.

She danced until sweat ran down her chest and off her forehead, until she felt dangerously dehydrated. Stopping to grab a drink would've made sense, but bottles of water were selling for three dollars, not that much less than an acid trip.

After what Trix guessed was a few hours, a bunch of people had coupled up. Many were alone like her, though, just grooving to the sounds.

Marjorie and Isaac had disappeared.

The light show was starting to make Trix dizzy and she knew she needed to find water. She decided to spend the three bucks on a bottle, but by then couldn't find anyone selling it.

A new DJ took the stage, a guy wearing all white, with long blond hair. Trix couldn't tell any difference between his music and the last DJ's.

She knew she'd be at the party for a while yet, at least until Marjorie and Isaac came off their trip and emerged from whatever corner they'd slipped off to. She tried to keep going with the beat.

Before long, the room began to spin. *Ignore it. Just dance. Pretend you're drunk or high.* She waved her glow sticks and wiped sweat from her forehead. She told herself her brain wasn't swirling like sand in a windstorm. She just needed to watch for the water person.

Then it happened. Trix felt herself going down, the rafters and people and music draining from her consciousness in a whirl of confusion.

She opened her eyes. She was outside, lying on asphalt, looking up into the black night sky. She heard the occasional rumble of a car, but was otherwise alone. She sat up slowly. Her clothes were intact, thank God.

What the hell had happened? She'd been thirsty. So thirsty. Dizzy. Beyond that, though, she couldn't recall anything. She must've gotten dehydrated and passed out. People at the party probably thought she was having a bad trip and didn't want to get in trouble so they moved her outside?

Where was Marjorie? Why hadn't she stuck by her, at least? Gotten her in Isaac's car and taken her home?

Then it occurred to her, as she sat alone on the shoulder of a street deep in SODO, that Marjorie could be in worse shape than she was, that Marjorie really had taken drugs. Either that or she was just too caught up in her fun to have noticed Trix.

Angry, she stood. She was still parched, still dizzy. It was cold and she had only her tank top on. Rubbing her arms, she began walking.

A car passed slowly, its brake lights flaring. It reversed.

A man, obviously drunk and older than her father, stuck his head out the window and slurred, "You lost? 'Cuz you looks lost."

"No!" she barked.

"Ok," he said and shook his head. "S'ok. I jus' thought I'd help if you're needing directions."

"I'm fine," she said. She turned her back to him and continued on. She knew she'd find a bus stop somewhere.

The car, a low-riding Buick, pulled up on her again.

"You wantin' a ride, pretty girl?"

"No!" she yelled again. "No, thanks. My, uh, my boyfriend is picking me up in a minute. He's a cop," she lied.

"Oh yeah? Them's good guys. Saved my poor ass more 'an once." Gold flashed inside his mouth.

Trix was still walking and the car was still puttering slowly next to her. She supposed she should've been scared. She was in SODO alone at night. But there was something amiable about the guy. He wasn't going to grab her and throw her in the backseat. He wasn't going to try to get her naked and hurt her. Somehow she knew this.

"Okay, well you take care, girl. You call that cop boyfriend a yours and tell 'im down here in the dark ain't no place for a pretty thang."

Sighing and allowing herself a half smile, she said, "I will."

"Good deal. Awright now. You take care," he said again. The car rumbled off, the window still open.

Trix thought about Marjorie again. She wasn't feeling very charitable toward her newish cohort at the moment. It was becoming clear that, with Marjorie, fun would always trump friendship.

44. CONFRONTATION

THE NEXT MORNING Emily spotted Trix again. They were walking toward each other on the school's second floor. At first Emily didn't know who was coming along, just thought it was someone from her class. But then the high heels, ripped sweater, and leopard-print belt came into focus. She noticed a hesitation in Trix's gait and wondered, briefly, if she'd turn and walk the other way.

Trix kept coming though and said, "Hey." She walked on as if Emily were any old person, not her best friend for the past five years.

Emily stopped and said. "Wait."

Trix didn't want to wait. She didn't have the energy for a conversation with Emily. But she gave in, pausing, and turning slowly.

"Trix ... " Emily didn't know what to say.

"Yeah, what?"

"You're not you, lately," Emily said. "What's going on? Can you please tell me? Because I'm at a total ... loss."

Trix's eyes had a hardness to them. A red- and blackness.

"I'm still me," she said. She was, she thought. Just a more experienced version of herself. Whoever the hell that was.

"You're a different you, then. One I didn't know was in there."

Crossing her arms, Trix scowled and focused hard on the glass display case that the Spanish club had put together. It held a mini sombrero, Mexican worry dolls, a package of tortillas (which was just weird), and a one-page story written in Spanish that she had never seen anyone actually standing there reading. "Yeah, well," Trix said.

Then Emily took the risk and said, "You wanna hang out? I'm at Shutter Ho after school, but I'll have a break around four thirty. We could have a quick cup." Shutter Ho was what Emily and Trix used to jokingly call Emily's workplace.

Without looking directly at Emily, Trix said, "Okay. I guess."

"Great. First and Vine. Remember?"

Trix nodded, then went up to the glass case and said, "Why are there freaking tortillas in there? In case the dolls get the munchies?"

Emily laughed. Laughed with relief. She laughed at Trix's ability to say what Emily was thinking, but in a much funnier way than Emily ever could.

MORE THAN ANYTHING, Emily wanted to be able to report that she and Trix met for coffee, hugged and cried, and opened up to each other again.

But that wasn't what happened. Seeing how Trix came into the coffee shop—her posture so intentionally loose she might as well have blurted that this was no big deal to her and she didn't know why she was there—punctured Emily's hopes right away.

She fetched Americanos for them both, black for Trix, cream for herself, and realized that communicating with her was going to be like chipping away at a rock with a cotton ball.

Emily was suddenly sorry she'd invited Trix. Shutter Ho had become a haven, of sorts, for her. She didn't love the idea of Trix's bitterness tainting the place.

"At least it's not Starbucks," Trix said.

For a minute, Emily thought she'd broken through. That Trix was remembering one of their inside jokes about bad art on coffee shop walls or the guy who'd once brought a blueberry pie into Café Obscura and proceeded to eat the whole thing.

"How's Frederick's?" Emily asked.

"Same old shithole as ever."

"Sorry."

"It's not your fault. If I could get a cushier job, one like this, that paid even half as much, I would," Trix said.

Envy, again, Emily thought. Was it new, or had she just never noticed it before?

After a minute, Trix said, "You should've seen Marjorie yesterday."

Deflated, Emily asked, "Why?"

"She's crossing the street, you know, out at 15th and 65th, and a car pulls up fast, like it's not gonna stop. So she turns to the driver, flashes her right boob and kicks the bumper. So funny."

Emily must've looked horrified, because Trix added, "I wouldn't expect you to get it."

"She sounds a little rough."

"That's what I like about her." Trix picked at the flaking black polish on her fingernails.

Suddenly a thunderclap of anger hit Emily. She saw, in front of her eyes, sparks of resentment and confusion and pissed offedness. "So, she's more in line with your current life philosophy," Emily said. "Treat people like they're trash unless you learn differently. I'm really happy for you, Trix. You and Marjorie are going places."

Trix's hackles raised visibly.

"Oh what?" she said. "Are you and Ryan going to get married? Have preppy little seven-foot long babies?"

"How would I know? I'm a junior in high school." This was not working out how Emily had wanted.

"Lots of people do it. Except ... oh wait ... I bet you haven't even had sex yet, have you?"

Emily glared at her ex-friend, who had turned so cruel and heartless. Or, maybe she'd always been that way, but had never directed it at Emily. She felt jealous herself then, of Marjorie. Marjorie was getting all the best of Trix while Emily had turned into *persona non grata*.

"Wouldn't you like to know?" Emily said.

Trix picked at her nails again, stretched her legs straight in front of her, one at a time. "Not especially."

Just then there was a crash. The shatter of porcelain. "Oopsie Daisy," Thomas called. He waved and tapped his watch. "Emmy, I need you, sunshine. Break's over."

He was rescuing her. She still had seven minutes of break left and they both knew it. But she was grateful. She stood, picked up her mug.

"Look," Trix said, leaning over the table so her breasts rested on the wood. "It's okay. Friends go different ways all the time."

"Not us."

"Yes, us."

"Am I that insufferable?" Emily asked.

Suddenly, Trix felt sorry for her old friend. Her eyes pleading, her big body hunched over. She forced her voice to soften as she said, "I think maybe I'm just not good enough for you."

45. The Meaningful Email

EMILY BROUGHT THE upstairs computer out of its sleep and got online. Her plan was to browse around, look for music, and maybe chat with Ryan if she could find him. But instead she wound up typing in the URL for the gallery where Marilyn Wozniak sold paintings.

There was her mother again. Thin-faced and frizzy-haired, smiling, her shoulder turned toward the camera. She wore a wide, colorful scarf that made you think of the Southwest. Peach and burnt orange with fringe. Hammered silver earrings dangled from her long lobes. Nothing about her contentedly set features betrayed that she'd once abandoned a husband and two little girls.

Emily pounded the keyboard with her fist. The monitor didn't even flicker. Anticlimactic.

She opened email and typed in her mother's address.

She was tempted to start it with *Hi Mom*. But decided that would be less funny than abrupt.

Hello there,

My name is Emily Lucas. I have a sister, Kristen Lucas. We were once your daughters. I guess technically we still are. Though we haven't heard from you in more than 11 years.

Emily backspaced. Too confrontational. She'd scare her away.

My name is Emily Lucas. I have a sister, Kristen Lucas. You're our mother.

I'm a junior at Cannon HS here in Seattle. I'm doing fine in school. I'm into photography and writing. I have a boyfriend, Ryan, who is almost too good to be true. But so far he is. True, I mean.

Turns out I'm really tall. Like, six-foot-and-counting tall. Dad is average height, as I'm sure you know. I can't remember, exactly, but you look tall to me. In your picture. And I've heard your father was extremely tall, too. Somehow it's nice for me to know that. Because I often feel like the only one. And I wonder how I ended up this way.

Kristen is normal and is ridiculously into sports. She's good at everything.

I'll keep this short. I just wanted you to know I'm out here and if you'd like to email me back, you can.

~Emily

She proofread her note and, before she could change her mind, hit send.

What on earth had she done?

THERE WAS NO reply from Marilyn Wozniak the next morning.

Emily felt the beginnings of regret in her gut. She shouldn't have emailed. It'd be so much easier to not have tried than to have reached out and gotten nothing in return.

And, even though there was no way Bob Lucas knew Emily had emailed Marilyn, he acted, that whole of Sunday, as if she'd somehow slighted him. He stomped around, yelled about spots on glasses and unmade beds, looked incessantly at his BlackBerry, and shot dirty looks to anyone who stared at him questioningly.

"It's work," Melissa told Emily. "Stocks are crashing. The market's bad."

When, in the last few years, hadn't the market been bad?

Kristen, wisely, was somewhere else.

Around noon, Emily decided she should leave, too. She actually wished it were a workday, but she was off on Sundays.

She took the bus down to Belltown anyway.

Just as she'd hoped, Thomas was at Shutter Ho by himself. "Can't stay away, can you?" he said, starting a latté for her.

"Apparently not." After being out in the cold, the café felt warm and dry. White lights lined the front windows and retro holiday songs played over the sound system.

"So, what's shakin'? Besides your boobies."

From anyone else, the remark would've deeply annoyed her, but she only laughed at Thomas, pulled up a tall stool behind the counter and said, "Too much." She confided Trix's antics, Emily's insecurities about her growth and how it could affect her relationship with Ryan, and her email to her mother.

Thomas looked at her with wide eyes, "Good for you! Every girl needs a mom."

"I don't know. I hope it was the right thing to do."

"It was, just you wait and see."

With a damp cloth, Thomas wiped down the Clover machine.

Emily was definitely in a funk. Even her time with Ryan lately had been tainted by regret that her increasing height would soon be too egregious for him to overlook.

The day before, Emily had talked him into going to Gasworks Park where they spread a blanket across the damp grass, planning to watch the winter sun set behind the city. But, too quickly, the ground's moisture soaked through the wool and they had to wad up their blanket, down their hot chocolate and peppermint schnapps, and trudge back to Ryan's car.

Things were weird between them and it wasn't just the fouled up plans.

Emily felt tentative, desperately wanting to ask what was going on but afraid of coming across as jumpy.

And Ryan. Ryan was a reserved, absent-minded version of himself. He would study Emily, looking at her for long, thoughtful moments during which she'd squirm and open her mouth to question him, then close it again, not sure what to say.

Back in the car, they listened to the radio and commented on songs they heard. When Ryan dropped Emily at her house, he said, "Sorry things didn't work out, Bean."

She gulped, not knowing, at first, what he meant.

"The sunset," he clarified. "I should've brought a plastic tarp."

"Oh," she said and shrugged. "It's okay."

He gave her a chaste kiss on the forehead and drove away.

Emily stood on the curb holding a reusable grocery bag filled with their thermoses and a Tupperware container of cookies she'd never gotten out, wondering what the heck was happening.

Sitting in the warm coffee shop, she made a mental list of her wants. She wanted … she wanted … what did she want? To stop growing. To wrap her arms around Ryan's shoulders and never let him go. To understand what happened with Trix. To establish a relationship with her mom.

Thomas disappeared into the back room and came out carrying three tall stacks of paper cups.

"Can I help with anything?" Emily asked.

"You just sit tight and tell me more about your man. What's he up to this weekend?"

Gloomily, she said, "He's skiing with friends at Crystal."

"You should learn to ski so you can go next time."

"I'm not really athletic. You know that."

A couple came in then, stamping off the cold and rubbing their palms together. Out the side of his mouth, Thomas said, "Is that why you're so down?"

Once he'd made the couple's drinks, he turned to her. "I mean, you look a little sick, hon."

"I just … as much as I try to tell myself otherwise, I feel like he's only mine for a little while. Something's going to tear us apart," she muttered.

"Like what?"

She relayed her conversation with Kennedy.

"Do you think he wants to be stolen?"

"I don't know," Emily fiddled with a metal tamper, rocking it back and forth in her palm.

The couple left the shop, letting in a gust of icy air. Thomas said, "It's your job to make sure he knows what a fabulous catch you are. Don't let him forget."

Embarrassed, Emily looked down at her big feet perched on a rung of the stool. She wished she felt as fabulous as Thomas thought she was.

46. WORSE THAN NOTHING

BY THE TIME Emily got home, darkness pooled around the bases of trees, seeped into the grass, and hung in the air. Her dad had cloistered himself in his office. Melissa baked banana-nut-oat bread. Kristen was still gone somewhere. And a reply from Marilyn Wozniak waited in Emily's inbox.

Her breath caught and she clicked.

Dear Art Aficionado,

Thank you for your interest in my work. I will respond to you as soon as possible. In the meantime, thank you for supporting Southwest artists.

Best,

Marilyn Wozniak

Emily closed her eyes and shook her head, willing her nervous system to relax. It was a form email. Nothing. Worse than nothing, it had pumped her full of temporary hope. She was only sixteen and already so many regrets. Why had she ever contacted her mom?

Emily remembered a conversation she'd had with Kristen a few months ago, where her optimistic sister tried to convince them both that their mother having left wasn't that big of a deal. They still had their dad, a decent stepmom and a nice big house to live in.

To Emily, though, losing their mom was something that stuck with her every day. It hid between the clothes in her closet, slept in bed with her at night, squeezed into her desk chair, and hissed into her ear: *Your mom left because you weren't lovable enough.*

47. SLIPPING AWAY

WHEN EMILY GOT to school Monday morning, Ryan was not waiting by the bike rack as he often did. He wasn't hovering near her locker, either. She saw him in his normal seat in Johnson's English class, though. She was sure her face was bright red as she slipped into her old desk.

Trix was MIA, of course.

Emily opened her notebook and pretended to study something intently until Johnson stepped into the classroom with a handful of papers fresh off the copier and started talking about expository essays.

Emily couldn't focus. All she could think about was what would transpire, or not, between Ryan and her after class. She was barely even conscious of the Farkettes sitting off to her left.

Johnson looked, to her, like a large puppet moving his mouth without producing sound.

Please let Ryan come up to me and apologize for being out of touch and kiss me in the hallway.

She watched clouds swirl past the window until the bell rang. She didn't want to obviously wait for him, so she slowly gathered her things, pretending to have lost her pencil.

He approached. "How was your weekend?"

So it hadn't been just her imagination. His voice was remote, as if he stood at the end of a long pipe. "Okay," she said, suddenly on guard. Though she was also aware that her own voice had turned a little whiny. "Surprised I didn't hear from you, is all."

He rubbed his forehead. "I know. Sorry."

"It's okay," she said, without meaning it.

She noticed Kennedy Furukawa sliding past her, taking in Emily and Ryan's interaction.

"History next?" he antiseptically asked.

"Yeah, history next."

He started to leave the room and Emily followed.

In the hallway, he turned. "Can we have lunch together?"

Her heart leapt. Until he added, "I need to talk to you."

She agreed, then headed off to her next class. She slogged her way through the morning, wishing she could stop time so she wouldn't have to hear Ryan break her heart, or speed it forward to get the bloodbath over with. By the time lunch rolled around, she had a stomach-ache.

They met at the bike racks and agreed to go to a barbeque place a few blocks down where they wouldn't see as many kids as at Fatty's.

The moment they'd ordered and taken a table, Emily said, "What, Ryan?"

With a straw, he jabbed at the ice in his Coke. He looked up at her and his eyes were damp.

Emily would've felt sorry for him, but she was pretty sure she knew what was coming. "You're breaking up with me, aren't you?"

He sighed, slumped back in his seat and said, "You know I think you're great, right?"

"I thought I did." She sat with her arms tucked protectively around her stomach. She couldn't believe this was happening.

"Well, you are."

So why the sad eyes? She wanted to ask. *Why are you tormenting me like this?*

"But?"

He shook his head and a small smile lit his lips. "You're making this too easy for me. You should just pretend that everything's fine and make me drop the bomb. Instead you're pulling it out like one of those magician's scarves."

"Except that I can't. Pretend everything's fine."

A twenty-something guy in a black sweater and jeans delivered their food. Neither Ryan nor Emily could look at it, much less eat it.

"I know," he said. "You're not a game player. That's one of the things I dig about you."

She considered asking if he wanted to date someone else, but no. He was right. She was making this too easy on him. If he was seeing another girl, he was going to have to tell her.

"The thing is," he began. "Well, there are a few things."

Emily pushed her plate away and stared at the CHS logo on Ryan's t-shirt. She would not cry. She would not cry.

He began to jiggle his knee. "The first thing," he said. "is how you act when you're with me. Kinda like you don't want to be there. It's like you've pulled away."

"What?" she cried. "No!"

"It's just a feeling I get."

"I haven't! Not on purpose. I was afraid that you were pulling away from me. I've been hearing things."

His eyebrows jacked up and he looked nervous. "You have?"

She decided to just tell him. To lay the truth out there. What did she have to lose at this point? "I heard someone was trying to … lure you away from me. And then there's my weirdo family—"

"We all have weirdo families," he said.

"I know, but, my dad. He's so strict." She still couldn't bring herself to mention her lack of a mother. "And then, there's, you know, how tall I am." *Why am I giving him reasons to dump me?* She wondered. *I'm too nice. I'm too damn nice.*

He gave a sideways nod as if he were conceding her height was an issue. *Oh God*, she thought. *It is.*

Trying to infuse his voice with kindness, which only came across as condescension, he asked, "How tall are you now?"

Emily buried her face in her hands. "You're dumping me because I'm six foot, aren't you?"

"No, Em. No," he reached across and grabbed her arm. She jerked it back.

"I thought you were different," she said. He'd found someone petite and girly. Someone he could feel like a man with. "Who is it?"

"It's no one."

She could tell he was lying. His eyes had gone all squinty and he wouldn't look at her. "The least you can do is be honest." A horrible thought came to her. "Is it Trix?"

His face contorted angrily now. "God, no. She's hella messed up. Be careful of her, Em. She's no good for you."

"Oh, and you know what's good for me, now." *You're good for me*, she wanted to say. *Or, you were.*

An older couple came in with a small dog whose nails clicked across the concrete floor. Emily took a token sip of Diet Coke, then proceeded to hold her finger over one end of the straw suctioning up soda and letting it go over the ice. Hot tears stung the corners of her eyes and she couldn't stop them. She felt like she was sitting across from a different person. She wanted Ryan back. Her Ryan.

She suddenly knew she had to get out of there, that she couldn't sit across from him and have that conversation for one more second. She stood and jammed her arms through her backpack's straps.

"Wait, Em," he said, but his voice was absent any sort of conviction.

"See you around," she said and scurried away before her chin began to quiver and she fell to pieces.

Emily raced up the street, away from school. She rushed past house after house with small detached garages and dead plants in the yards. She barely felt the drizzle pinging her face or heard the barking of dogs.

Ryan did not chase her. She realized this with a simultaneous sense of relief and disappointment.

After a few blocks, she slowed and looked around. Salmon Bay Park, where she used to play as a kid, was to her left. Dejectedly, she ambled over to a swing and sat down. The rubber was wet and the dampness quickly soaked through her jeans. She didn't care. She didn't care about anything right then.

The best thing that had happened to her in high school, or ever, had ended. She looked down at her long legs stretched before her on the swing and was disgusted. Just a few inches. If only she were a few inches shorter.

Damn her tallness. Damn her absentee mother for passing down the tallness. It sucked to tower over everyone, weaving down the school halls like a sailboat mast caught in a hard wind, trying her best to blend when blending wasn't possible.

Wood chips clumped in wet piles under her feet.

She imagined that if Melissa could see her now, she'd sympathetically ask if Emily was done feeling sorry for herself yet.

"No," she said aloud to the empty playground. "As a matter of fact, I'm not."

She shivered and tried to withdraw further into her sweatshirt. She suddenly ached to be home, in her room, wrapped in a thick fleece blanket, drinking something hot, and listening to sad music.

Standing slowly, she started back to school. She wished she could call Trix. Nothing would be better, right then, than hearing her profanity-laced take on Ryan's recent assholery. But Trix wasn't on her side. Trix was jealous and insecure and done with Emily.

48. SADNESS/HOPE/REMORSE

AVOIDING RYAN THE rest of the day wasn't hard. He'd made himself scarce. After school, she unlocked her bike alone, imagining other kids from her class whispering, nudging. *Did you hear that Big Bird got dumped today? It was only a matter of time.*

At home, she avoided Melissa and Kristen and burrowed into bed, where she let pent up tears drown her.

Later, after she'd refused dinner, gotten into her pajamas at eight thirty and snapped on the upstairs computer, she found an email from Kennedy Furukawa.

I heard what happened with Ryan today. Super annoying. We should meet up for coffee this week. Thursday?
Best, K.F.

Awesome. Just what Emily needed. One of the Farkettes setting her up for some cruelty, maybe a briefing on who Ryan was dating now.

The house smelled like the patchouli wax chips that Melissa burned in a small saucepan on the stove. Emily's dad bellyached that it made the place reek of a hookah lounge, but Melissa let the wax bubble and waft anyway.

Emily wouldn't answer Kennedy's email just yet. She had some thinking to do.

She watched a few videos on YouTube, checked her favorite sites, and zipped through her Facebook newsfeed. There was absolutely nothing from Ryan. No, *Oh Crap. I don't know what I was thinking today! I have to see you now!* No forwarded jokes or posted photos.

But just as Emily was about to sign out, a new message flicked to the top of her inbox. It was from Marilyn Wozniak. *Re: I think I know you.*

Emily swallowed hard. She was tempted to get Kristen so they could read it together. She wanted so badly to let her in on the secret: that she knew the whereabouts of their mother and had contacted her. But Kristen seemed happy and well adjusted. Why knock a hole in that?

If she were honest with herself, she was also a little afraid Kristen would thwart her somehow, talk her out of communicating with Marilyn.

Emily briefly considered deleting the email without reading it .
Why today? What the hell?

But then … all she had to do was click once to read words her mother had composed. To Emily. She may, in the email, ask Emily never to contact her again, but whatever she'd written, she'd written to her. Assuming it wasn't another form letter from the gallery.

Anxiety welled up in her chest like a third lung. She waved her hands in front of her face, as if this would help her breathe, and clicked the message.

Dear Emily,

Did you know your name means Rival. Laborious. Eager? Yes, your father picked that one out.

Thanks for emailing me. I've wondered about you and your sister often over the years.

To answer your question, I am just shy of six feet tall. I am married to a wonderful man, Winslow, who is six ten! He reminds me a lot of my own father.

Do you have a photo of you and Kristen?

"Do not be too moral. You may cheat yourself out of much life. So aim above morality. Be not simply good; be good for something".
~Henry David Thoreau

Marilyn Wozniak

At the bottom of her message, she'd attached a photo of one of her paintings. Or, what Emily assumed to be one of her paintings. It was a wolf standing on a cliff, howling into the sunset. The strokes were colorful and bold.

Emily felt let down. The message was too short and sterile. But then, what had she expected? Pronouncements of love and regret? An offer of a plane ticket so Emily could fly to Arizona for a visit? This was a woman capable of leaving two young daughters. A woman who hadn't sent a single birthday card in the past twelve years.

And the Thoreau quote? Good God. Marilyn Wozniak was out of touch. Worse, she was delusional. *Yes, don't worry about being good, Marilyn. Don't worry your frizzy little head about doing what's right.*

Emily started crying and could not stop. Not even when Melissa knocked on her bedroom door with offers of smoothies and peanut butter/sprout sandwiches. She came back a second time saying she'd toasted Emily a Pop-Tart and made her hot chocolate. Emily could only respond with a choked, "No, thanks."

When she'd calmed enough to breathe, she called Thomas. She told him about the break up and the barren email from Marilyn. He was enjoying a rare day off, shopping a late night sale at Nordstrom. He clucked sympathetically and tried to talk her into meeting him so they could look for jeans together.

Emily declined. She couldn't have cared less about clothes right then.

"I just needed to talk to a friend," she said.

"Anytime, babe. Night or day."

This made her smile a little. She was grateful for Thomas.

Later, when Kristen jimmied Emily's lock with a paperclip and stood in her doorframe, yellow light from the hallway pouring in around her, Emily only turned swollen eyes in her direction and grunted.

"You're scaring me, Em. What's wrong?"

"Close the door!" Emily yelled.

So, Kristen did. But she stayed inside Emily's bedroom. "I'm not leaving."

Emily rolled over and pulled a pillow on top of her head.

"What happened today?"

"Lots of things." Emily's voice was muffled and full of contempt. She did not want to say any of the day's catastrophes out loud. Least of all to her always-together sister.

"Well, can you be more specific?" Kristen asked, coming over and sitting on the edge of Emily's mattress.

"Not really."

Wind buzzed through the window screens and rattled the house's siding.

Kristen, wisely, sat still and didn't say a word.

Finally, Emily took the pillow from her head and said, "Do you really want to know?"

"Duh. Why else would I be in here?"

"Okay." Emily took a deep, shuddering breath. "Ryan dumped me."

"Oh, Em."

"And Mom emailed me."

She heard Kristen gasp. "What do you mean 'Mom' emailed you?" She made air quotes around the word "Mom." Her expression was a mix of horror and hope.

There was a gust of wind so powerful that the whole house shook. Emily said, "I found her online and emailed her. She emailed me back."

"What'd she say?" Kristen yelped, agitatedly cracking her knuckles.

"Not much." Emily filled her in on the content of Marilyn's email.

"That quote–What the hell?" Kristen cried.

"I know."

Kristen jumped up from where she'd been sitting on the bed. "Did she ask anything about us and our lives? Did she apologize?"

Emily's throat was scratchy and she badly needed a drink of water. "No, none of that."

"What is her problem?" Kristen bellowed. She stood in the middle of the room with her hands on her hips. Emily hadn't seen her sister so worked up in years. Not since Emily had borrowed Kristen's bike in middle school, run over a nail, and forgotten to tell her about it until Kristen was ready to set off on Schwinn with her friends. "The woman gave birth to us! And she doesn't even care? She doesn't even wonder?"

"I know."

"Something's wrong with her."

"Uh, yeah."

Emily got up and moved across her room like a massive, wobbling bubble that hadn't yet popped. She retrieved a glass of water from her and Kristen's shared bathroom and took it back to bed.

Sipping, she said, "She's selfish. She's a narcissist. We just have to accept it."

Kristen folded to the floor, looking wounded. "We already knew that. Why'd you have to find her and confirm it again?" she asked softly.

"I'm sorry."

They sat there silently, wind thrashing the trees and house.

"And Ryan," Kristen said. "What happened?"

"I'm too tall. Too mopey. I think he's seeing someone else."

Kristen walked on her knees over to Emily's mattress. She laid her head on Emily's leg. "I'm sure it's not that you're too tall."

Emily felt wracking sobs overtake her again. She just managed to squeak, "I could really use a hug right now."

As her sister embraced her, Emily wondered what, when she was done wallowing, her next step would be. Email Marilyn? Fight for Ryan? Or just sit back and let her fate unfold?

49. Applying Herself

TRIX STARED NUMBLY at the sheaf of papers in her hands. It was an application to The Art Institute of Seattle. Her guidance counselor had given it to her and suggested that Trix would have enough credits to graduate at the end of junior year if she wanted to.

The Art Institute had a fashion degree program. Thinking about applying excited Trix. It was, in fact, the one thing getting her through the throes of her current Down. She was coming off a night out with Marjorie where Trix had slept with another guy she didn't know or particularly like.

She'd met him at a basement party. This is what she remembered about him: he was Asian with beautifully sculpted cheekbones, a dainty chin, and wild mohawk that looked less stiff than moppy. He said hardly anything, but pulled her onto a coffee table with him and danced.

When it tipped and they both fell onto a sofa, they started to make out. Literally no words exchanged until they'd moved to a back room and she asked if he had a condom.

She'd felt special, in those fifteen minutes they'd been dancing. He'd chosen her out of all the other girls in the room. And, though his eyes had barely met hers and he didn't say anything, their bodies moved rhythmically with the music and she had erroneously sensed that they were in tune, communicating on a level higher than words. But then, it could've been all the vodka tonics she'd consumed.

Stupid, she thought. *Stupid, stupid drunk girl. Again.*

Underneath her, the bus rumbled up Fifteenth Avenue.

She was on her way to her shift at Frederick's. She avoided the break room now and instead took her twenty minutes outside, sitting on a small strip of grass along the road smoking or, if it was rainy, standing under an eave.

The feeling of waking up that morning and knowing she'd added another notch to her metaphorical bedpost had been miserable. There was no way to describe the sensation except *gross*. She'd assumed, once upon a time, that if a girl slept with many, many guys it would become rote. Boring. Un-upsetting. But, no. If anything, every time Trix did it, she felt deeper remorse. Dirty. Unworthy of the good people of the world. Which perpetuated itself, because the next time she went to a party and got drunk on alcohol and the attention of a boy, she'd think, *Why not? I'm a loser anyway.*

She looked down at the papers on her lap. The words blurred together as if they were underwater. Which they sort of were. Trix realized her eyes had filled.

What made her think she could get into the Art Institute, or, if she made it, afford tuition? Okay, so, if she started trying again she could easily ace the academic stuff, the books and memorization that was high school. She could get loans, too, she supposed.

She needed confidence to prove her creative talent, though. And, in that moment, her self-assurance was at an all-time low.

No more boys, she told herself. No more partying or hooking up. She needed to pull herself together and focus.

The question was, could she?

50. Tricky Times

MELISSA JUMPED AROUND the living room to a Jillian Michaels DVD. Emily lay on the couch watching her and sipping a chai latté that Melissa had brought back from a morning walk to Tully's.

"You know," Melissa said, only slightly out of breath. "When someone falls out of our lives, I think it's for a reason. To make room for new people."

The storm of the night before had subsided into a gray, drippy day, just like so many other gray, drippy days in the Pacific Northwest.

Emily refused to believe that a cosmic force had nudged Ryan out of her life so she could meet someone even more fabulous. He'd been perfect. Or as close to perfect as any girl could reasonably expect.

She was beginning to suspect that Kennedy was right, Ryan's termination of the relationship was the work of underhanded high school girls. She didn't know how or why, but she felt it in her bones.

She grunted at Melissa, who was now lying on the ground with her feet together, at a ninety-degree angle to her torso. She lowered one leg, then the other and brought them back up.

"I mean, like Trix," Melissa said. "It took her stepping aside so you could spend time with Ryan. And now someone else gets a chance with you." Melissa was on a mid-workout high, giddily spouting platitudes because she couldn't help herself.

"And, like, my mom had to leave so my dad could meet you and bring you to us," Emily said. Her voice snagged on the word "leave" and slid into haughty insolence.

"Right!" Melissa chirped, but her gaze shifted doubtfully toward Emily.

Emily muttered, "I thought Ryan was better than that."

"The teens are tricky times."

"You get an A for alliteration."

Melissa ignored Emily's jab and continued, "You know, good people sometimes do and say things they'll later wish they hadn't. Trust me on that."

"You think he'll regret dumping me?"

"Of course!"

Emily watched Melissa finish her workout and down two glasses of water at the kitchen sink. She then wandered up to the shower.

After watching a few episodes of a show about teen moms, which was the modern version of Jerry Springer, Emily hoisted herself off the sofa and went to get ready for work. She hoped Shutter Ho would be busy that day. So busy she wouldn't have time to think.

51. TRIPTYCH

A WEEK UNTIL Christmas. For the first time Emily could remember, she didn't care at all. There was none of the excitement from years past. No pleasant lifting of her stomach as she wondered what she might get or anticipation over watching her family open presents she'd given. Numbness had overtaken her.

She would, however, be infinitely grateful for the holiday break. To not have to be at school seeing Ryan and Trix drifting through the hallways would be a relief. Maybe by the time she went back in early January she'd be over Ryan. Or more over him than she was right then. Which wasn't at all.

It was on that day, seven days before Christmas, that she decided to email Marilyn Wozniak back.

But, as she sat down to send a message, she found herself checking airfares to Arizona instead. She'd saved enough money from her job that she could afford the trip. And nothing sounded better, right then, than leaving cold and rainy Seattle for the desert.

Her heart thudded in her ears as she came upon a last minute deal. Three hundred and twenty dollars for a round-trip flight. Provided she was willing to leave Christmas Eve. Now, her obstacles. How to convince her dad this was a good idea? Where to stay? And should she tell Marilyn she was coming or surprise her?

Was she really thinking about doing this?

After a little more searching, and with shaking fingers, she booked herself in a youth hostel for the first night, hoping (probably foolishly) that she could stay with Marilyn for the second and third nights. She put the plane ticket on hold until she could plead with her dad for permission and his credit card number that night.

There was still a lot standing between her and meeting Marilyn Wozniak.

"WHY NOT?" EMILY asked her dad as she stood behind him in his home office. The room was starkly masculine with slate blue walls and a huge, dark wooden desk. She swore she could smell his golf clubs—metallic and rubbery.

She'd found him just a few minutes before, typing away on his laptop, and she'd come right out and asked. Could she go visit her mother for Christmas? And would he loan her his credit card? She'd withdraw the cash tomorrow to pay him back.

At first, he'd been flustered. "Your mother? What do you mean *visit your mother*? We don't even know where she is."

Defiantly lifting her chin the slightest bit, she said, "I do." She explained how she'd found Marilyn, how they'd communicated (though she didn't tell him the sum total of their email exchanges were one each).

"No," he'd boomed. "No way. You can't fly down there by yourself and stay with some flighty artist who isn't to be trusted."

"Lots of kids fly by themselves. Thousands. Besides, it's not like I'm eight. I'm sixteen."

"No, Emily. End of story. Case closed. It's a ridiculous idea."

She watched his profile for any sign that her request to visit Marilyn had hurt him. But his face gave nothing away: no tick of his cheek or tug of his brows.

She considered groveling. Whining. Bawling. But she knew none of it would work. Her father, once he'd made up his mind, was impossible to sway.

Lowering her voice to almost a whisper, she said, "Please."

"How many times do I have to say 'No'?" Throughout the discussion/argument, her father had never once turned to look at her.

Chest burning, she said, "All right, fine." But it wasn't fine, and she hadn't given up the idea of going to visit her real mom for Christmas.

SUNLIGHT FLOODED EMILY'S room. She peeled off her coat and tossed it on her bed, then flopped down next to it to flip through the photos on her camera.

She'd shot neighbors' Christmas lights, plastic cutouts of snowmen, and Santas all glinting garishly in the midday light.

She'd snapped photos of cigarette butts languishing on lampposts, a colorful party hat, flattened to the wet pavement, and leafless trees etched across the gray sky.

A few of the shots were crisp and stark. Exactly what she'd been going for. But others just kind of limped, muddy and ill-composed.

There was a quiet tap on her door that Emily recognized as Melissa's skinny knuckles. She always knocked softly, almost inaudibly.

"Yeah? What?" Emily snapped.

"Can I come in?"

Letting loose a huge, put-out sigh, Emily stood and swung the door open. "What?" She cocked her hip and looked down at Melissa.

Melissa gently shouldered her way past Emily. "Close the door," she whispered.

Emily did as she was told, quietly clicking it shut.

Melissa's face was strained, her eyes worried. "Here," she said. She handed Emily an American Express card. It was smooth and cool in Emily's palm. She ran her finger over the raised numbers and looked at Melissa questioningly.

"So you can go visit your mother," Melissa said.

"Really? But … you don't have to—"

"I know I don't. And your dad's probably going to divorce me for this. But you should. You should be able to figure this out. And if that means you need to have a face-to-face with Marilyn, you ought to."

Hearing Melissa say Marilyn's name sent a cold purl up Emily's spine. "I don't want Dad to be mad at you, too."

"I'll deal with him."

"I can't believe you're doing this."

"I know."

"Thank you."

Melissa crossed her arms and shook her head. "You know, your dad loves you."

"Sometimes I find that hard to believe."

"He's been through some things, too. That make him the way he is now. I'm sure you've heard this, but his family didn't have much money when he was a kid."

"So poor they had to poop in a hole in the woods. That's what he's always told us."

"Right," Melissa said. "He never wants you girls to have to go through that. And Marilyn's leaving ... that really hurt him."

Nodding, Emily said, "Can I ask you a question?"

"Sure."

"What do you see in him? I mean, what's the big draw? He's unpleasant so much of the time. Like, mean."

Melissa's face softened. "I don't see him as mean."

Emily kept her voice low and respectful because Melissa was doing this amazing thing for her, helping her find her mother. But she wanted to jump on the bed and shriek. "Like how? What then?"

"Bob really helped me. I was in debt, living in a crummy apartment in Rainier Beach. And, I'm going to tell you something almost no one knows ... "

She hesitated for such a long time Emily thought Melissa had changed her mind about telling her secret.

Finally, Melissa said, "I had just had a miscarriage when I met your dad."

"What?"

Looking her straight in the eyes, Melissa said, "Yep. A boyfriend got me pregnant. I had mixed feelings about the whole thing, but in the end decided I really wanted to keep the baby. Unfortunately, though, I lost it."

Emily forced her jaw closed. "And you broke up with the boyfriend right after?"

"I realized there wasn't much keeping us together." Melissa said. "Anyway, I was kind of broken and your dad helped me pick up the pieces."

"Is that why you're so devoted to him?"

"That and he's a good man. He is, Em. I see that derisive glint in your eye. He works too hard and loses sight of what's important sometimes, but he wants the best for all of us."

"Wow," Emily said. "I had no idea. About your ... about what happened to you."

Melissa said, "Now, I'm assuming your mother has made arrangements to pick you up at the airport."

Oh God. Emily was going to have to lie. And after Melissa had been so generous. After she'd confessed her past. But if she told the truth, that Marilyn Wozniak had no idea her daughter was coming on Christmas Eve, Melissa would grab her card back like a frog snatching an insect out of the air.

"Yes," Emily said. "She and her husband, Winslow."

"Do I need to contact her?"

"No! No. It's covered."

"You have to call me when you get there. And twice a day until you come home."

Emily was breathless. This was really going to happen. "I will. I promise."

"And I want you to email me your itinerary."

"Yes, of course."

"Okay, you have the airport shuttle pick you up a few blocks away. I'll track your flight online and once you've taken off, I'll tell your father."

Both anguished and relieved, Emily said. "Oh, God."

"I know. It'll be ugly. Not a very merry Christmas, I imagine. But we'll survive."

Emily went to Melissa and hugged her. "Thank you," she said into Melissa's shiny black hair. "Thank you so much."

Melissa hugged her back, an almost desperate grip, her fingernails digging into Emily's shoulder blades.

"Oh," Emily pulled away and went to her dresser. She took $350 from a small lacquered box and handed the wad of money to her stepmom.

Melissa took it, but did not count it. She shoved it into her pocket.

"I hope this is worth it," Melissa said.

Emily took a deep breath and said, "Me too."

52. FEAR AND LOATHING ON THE DARK SIDE

TRIX SLOGGED THROUGH the next few days, wondering why the heavy feeling of regret wasn't evaporating like it usually did. Normally, after giving it up to a boy, she felt slutty and cheap for a day, maybe two. But, then she vowed not to do it again and eventually regained her equilibrium. This time, the remorse was a steel-gray mist hanging around her, trailing her, making it hard for her to concentrate on studying.

Once, after school, she tried to talk to Marjorie about it. They were walking through Fremont drinking espressos and deciding how to score some cigarettes without actually buying them, when Trix brought it up. "When you ... have sex with a guy, do you ever wish you hadn't?"

Marjorie looked at her squinty-eyed. "What do you mean?"

"Do you feel ... nasty?"

"Absolutely not. We need to own our sexuality, okay? Guys go around sticking their dicks in anything that breathes, but if we want to have unattached sex we're supposed to feel trashy? Nuh-uh."

"All guys don't stick it in anything."

"Oh really? I don't buy that."

Trix knew it was true, though. Ryan, for instance, was a good one. He wasn't in it just to see what he could get.

Still, Marjorie's words made Trix feel better. She was right. If guys could have sex with no strings, so could girls.

They went into a store called Bliss and tried on a few dresses. Marjorie walked out with one in her purse, plus a pair of earrings for Trix.

"You're bad," Trix said.

"I know," Marjorie cackled. "And you worship me for it."

Trix thought about this. She'd always considered herself pretty brazen, until she met Marjorie and realized she was just a hack in the presence of a true crazy person. Did she wish she were more like Marjorie? Only in the way that Marjorie *owned* everything she did without regret or remorse. That Trix did admire.

But Marjorie's dark side was several shades darker than Trix's, and it scared her a little. She didn't know what all her friend might attempt. And while that unpredictability could be fun, it also freaked Trix out.

She imagined telling Marjorie about Ryan and how bad and for how long she'd crushed on him. But Marjorie would laugh her head off at that one. Trix and straight-laced, *vanilla* Ryan. As if.

So Trix kept quiet, scratched at the imaginary ants skittering up her arms and legs, and slipped her new earrings into her pocket.

53. HELPLESS

LATER THAT NIGHT, Trix's mom called, asking if Trix could bring her some groceries.

"What?" Trix said. She'd been sitting at her dad's cheap Formica table, trying to study for an English Comp test while a WWF fight blared from the TV. She still had three chapters in her textbook to cover and half a novel to read. "You're not helpless, Ma. Go to Safeway."

"I'm sick," her mom said. "I've had to do three breathing treatments today."

"What about Rodney? Can't he bring you some Arby's?"

Her mom sighed, a long exhalation. "I need some vegetables, Trixie. Some carrots and apples or something."

Trix chewed the inside of her mouth to keep from exploding. She knew her mother wanted more than just the food. She wanted Trix to *buy* the food. From her Frederick's paycheck. She muttered a string of curse words under her breath. Trix only needed forty-six dollars more to get the sewing machine.

"Maybe tomorrow."

David came walking into the room and sat in front of her, blinking. She hauled him onto her lap and scratched his head.

"C'mon, Trixie. I could be dead by tomorrow. Safeway's open until midnight."

It was already ten o'clock, and a school night. She calculated that if she took the two buses it would require to get to the store, bought stuff for her mom, delivered it, and bussed it back to her dad's, she'd be home by midnight. One at the latest. And she still needed to get ready for the quiz tomorrow.

Her guidance counselor had informed Trix that any more unexcused absences or grades less than a C would result in her not graduating early. And getting out of school to start on her real life, hopefully at the Art Institute, sounded pretty appealing right then.

Still, it was hard to refuse Fiona. She was her mother, after all.

She began grumpily stuffing some clothes, makeup, and schoolbooks into her bag. "Okay, you know what? I'll bring you some food. But then I'm going to crash there, and I don't want to see Rodney. So, food or him?"

Her mother sighed as if Trix were ridiculous. "He's working tonight, Trixie."

"Okay, then."

On her way out, Trix stopped to tell her dad her plans, but he was asleep on the couch. She gingerly removed a half-full beer bottle from his hand, covered him with a thin blanket, and slipped out into the night.

54. SHOCK AND HORROR

IT WAS THE last day of school before holiday break and Emily pedaled her heavy bike east. She didn't know how to feel. Her emotions were like bricks. Ryan dumped her! She was going to see her mother! Ryan dumped her! She was going to see her mother!

She tried mightily not to let her breakup with Ryan ruin her upcoming trip to Bisbee. She'd been waiting so long to see her mother again. Far longer than she'd known Ryan.

Who knew? Maybe she and Marilyn would hit it off and drink iced tea together on her desert patio, trading photos and stories and memories.

It was a bitterly cold morning, though bright. When she rode, she had to visor a hand over her eyes to shield them from the low winter sun, and still she was afraid she'd mow over a pedestrian or get smacked by a turning car.

She was about four blocks from school, uneager to arrive but ready to be warm, when someone called her name.

Muttering to herself, "What now?" she turned to see Kennedy Furukawa sprinting toward her.

"Hey!" Kennedy said, out of breath. "I've been trying to catch up with you."

Emily waited reluctantly, decided she felt conspicuous in her helmet, and snapped it off.

"Any big plans for your break?" Kennedy asked, as if they were old friends.

Emily wasn't about to confide in Kennedy her plans of meeting her mother. "Not really, you?"

"We're going to Maui like we always do."

"Rough life."

"Yeah, well, my dad is half Hawaiian, so we see family."

Slowly, Emily started walking her bike alongside Kennedy. They continued their small talk, chatting about schoolwork they had to get done before they were set free on Friday. Finally, Kennedy got around to the reason she'd hunted down Emily, "So, Ryan."

Emily bit down hard on her bottom lip, then said, "We're not together anymore."

"I heard."

Of course Kennedy had heard. It was common knowledge by now.

"I think I can give you some insight into that."

"Into our breakup?"

They passed under a tree on which frosty pine needles trembled. A squirrel skittered across the sidewalk in front of them.

Emily said, "He told me why we broke up." Ryan dumped Emily because she was too tall, or too insecure about her tallness. Or something. Even as persistently decent as Kennedy was acting, Emily wasn't going to rehash it with her.

"Did he now?" Kennedy said.

"I mean, sort of. I stomped out halfway through his explanation."

"Well, there's more to the story than he probably told you."

"Okay. So it's your job to fill me in?"

"It's not my job. I want to. It's still mostly hush-hush except, you know, in our group."

Emily felt simultaneously crass and gnawingly, desperately curious. She was not part of "the group," and Kennedy deigning to share privileged information made Emily want to throw up in her mouth. But also to know.

"What then?" she said, irritability rising in her like a fast tide.

For a few moments, the only sound was their boots on dry concrete. Kennedy shifted her backpack and said, "Jessie Turner is claiming Ryan got her pregnant."

It was like someone had yelled, "Catch!" and thrown a twenty-pound bowling ball into Emily's soft, quivering gut.

She didn't realize she'd stopped walking until, several steps ahead, Kennedy turned and said, "I know, right?"

Emily's first thought was, *Jessie's lying.* Her second thought, really a question, was, *Did he get her pregnant before we got together or while he was with me?*

"I, uh, I'm processing ... " Emily said. She stared at her handlebar grips, at the brake cables that snaked down to the bike's wheels. She dug her fingernails into the spongy seat.

She had to put on her game face.

Slowly, she started moving again. "So, did he? Get her pregnant?"

"We don't know. He's too nice to claim the baby's not his if there's even a remote chance it is. There will be paternity tests once it's born."

"Is she keeping it?"

"She wants to."

"God." This seemed so much bigger now than just Emily's stature. Ryan was potentially going to be a parent. A dad, for cripe's sake. Yet she couldn't stop the nagging question from swimming around the forefront of her mind: Had he cheated on her? Emily asked, "How far ... how pregnant is she?"

"Five months."

Relief trickled through Emily. A bitter sort of relief. She and Ryan had only been together for two.

"It happened over the summer," Kennedy said, her lovely almond eyes shining with concern. "I'm sorry. I really just thought you deserved to know."

Emily should probably thank Kennedy, but couldn't bring herself to. "All right," was all she could muster.

After that, Kennedy launched into a tirade about their shared algebra class and all the equations they'd been assigned the night before. "I mean, that's the last thing I want to be doing. I'm trying to pack and shop for bikinis."

Emily couldn't switch gears that fast. So she remained mute. She thought she nodded in the appropriate places, but jumping into a conversation about math and swimsuits so soon after learning that Ryan had had sex with Jessie over the summer and might be a father was impossible.

When they came to the bike rack, Kennedy said, "See you in Johnson's class. By the way, did you hear about the Spring Spectacle?" It was a talent show Johnson was orchestrating. Facebook had been abuzz with it.

Emily nodded. She could not even begin to care about the Spring Spectacle.

"The stuff he comes up with," Kennedy called over her shoulder as she headed into school.

Emily managed a small wave.

She felt so naïve. So ridiculously sheltered. She knew Ryan had gone out with Jessie a while back, but obviously hadn't known they'd had sex. She didn't know much, as it turned out. But she did know she had to talk to Ryan.

55. I DON'T KNOW WHAT I KNOW

BETWEEN FIRST AND second period, Emily texted him.

Cn we talk?

He responded in less than 30 seconds.

Def. When?

Lunch?

Cant. Aftr schl?

Ok. Bike rck.

Coffee shp?

Fine. Obscura.

The day passed by in a blur of nausea and a pounding headache that began in PE and never let up. By the time she was locking her bike to a light pole on Market Street, she felt in danger of passing out.

She walked into the coffee shop. It was ambient with low, golden light fixtures and deep red walls. Ryan wasn't there yet, so she ordered a cup of mint tea to hopefully settle her stomach and took a small marble table far in the back.

Every time the door opened and cold air rushed in, she craned around to see if it was him. After fifteen minutes, she started to wonder if he was going to bug out completely.

She considered texting him but then, just as she was about to pull out her phone, he sidled up, his winter jacket swishing, and took the seat across from her.

They just looked at each other.

"Want a coffee?" Emily asked.

"Not now." He shook his head and rubbed his palms together. He was clearly nervous.

She was too. "So, are you wondering why I wanted to talk?"

"I think I have a pretty good idea why you wanted to talk."

Damn him for being so cute with his curly hair, strong nose and wide-set eyes. And his hands—long, tapered fingers, short, clean nails, slightly big knuckles. She could've cried. If she weren't so numb.

"Yeah," she said. "So, you and Jessie."

"Apparently," he said, looking miserable.

"I know about her ... condition."

He nodded.

"I mean, I did the math and I'm pretty confident you didn't ... impregnate Jessie while we were going out, but, did you—?"

"No, God! When you and I were together, there was no one else." His chin ticked and his hands visibly shook now.

Emily almost felt sorry for him. She crossed her arms and sat back in her chair. "Seriously? Because—"

"I swear," he said. "I hope you know I wouldn't do that."

"I don't know what I know!" Emily snapped. To get a grip, she gulped down some tea, burning her tongue in the process. "Is that why you broke up with me then? To be with Jessie?"

He stared at her, pleadingly, it seemed. He said, "I might be a dad, Bean."

"Please don't call me Bean."

"Sorry. Emily. A freaking dad. That would make Jessie the mom. What kind of guy would I be if I let her go through that alone?"

"You did ... have sex with Jessie over the summer then?" So bitter were the words to say, it was as if Emily had rolled raw cocoa beans around her mouth, then spit them into her palm.

He sighed. He jiggled his knee. "Once, at a beach bonfire. We were both soused. It was a mistake. I knew it was a mistake. But you and I were not together."

Maybe she and Ryan weren't going out at that point, but she hated imagining him with Jessie. He and Jessie had been together in a way he and Emily never would.

"Believe me," he said. "If this had to happen, I wish it were with you."

Her heart lifted, just a little.

His chin was full on quaking now. "I did not break up with you because you're tall or because your family's a little kooky or even because of any insecurities you had about me and us. But I couldn't tell you that then. I was totally shell-shocked and, stupidly, I was hoping this whole thing with Jessie would just go away and you and I could get back together at some point."

Emily said, "Really?"

"Yes!" He lowered his voice and between clenched teeth, said, "But I have to pretend I'm not totally wigged out and be supportive."

"So, you and Jessie are back together?"

"Technically we're boyfriend and girlfriend," he mumbled.

Wincing, Emily stared at the curve of their table. The gray and white flecks in the marble blurred into different shapes like clouds: a spaceship here, a giraffe there. She blew her nose into a scratchy paper napkin.

"Ugh," she said.

"Tell me about it."

Suddenly, it occurred to her to show some compassion. Jessie certainly hadn't been expecting this either. She'd be a sixteen-year-old mom, home changing diapers while everyone else was going out on weekends, running track, acting in school plays. At graduation, she'd have a toddler. "How's Jessie doing with it?"

"She's … a hard one to figure out. Some days she's totally pissed. Some days it seems like she's adjusting to the idea. And other days she acts like she wants it. Wants her, me, and the baby to be a happy family," Ryan said. He propped his chin on his palm. His eyes that used to dance and sparkle when he talked to her looked far away.

The air between them went dead. Small talk was inappropriate. She didn't know what else to say on the topic of Ryan's probable, impending fatherhood. And, frankly, sitting across from him like old times was making her irrepressibly sad.

"Well," she said.

"Well."

She was tempted to tell him about her upcoming Bisbee trip, but was also afraid to share another intimacy with him. If she filled him in, she'd want to update him. And she really needed to stay away. It wasn't like she was going to get him back. "I should go," she said, standing and gathering her stuff.

Ryan just sat there. "I'm gonna hang out here for a while."

And as she pushed out of the coffee shop, she turned, looked at the back of his curly head, and saw it hanging, his neck almost folded over on itself.

56. PRESSURE

HEAD POUNDING, TOTALLY exhausted, Trix sat slouched in her art history class. There was no doubt about it—her grades had slipped. Her guidance counselor had scheduled her for an emergency meeting that morning.

"As we discussed before, if you fail even one class," he'd said, "you won't be graduating early." He'd flipped through some papers on his desk. "And you're in danger of not passing English Comp."

Trix sat in the gray, plastic chair smelling his stale coffee and ink from the copy machine, and knew she wanted this. Graduating early was the key. It'd get her away from toxic high schoolers and in with talented kids who had goals. Plus, it'd move her one year closer to getting a real job and living on her own.

She imagined herself as an early twenty-something in New York. She'd have a little apartment, always stocked with bagels, coffee, rotisserie chicken, and chocolate milk. She'd invite friends over for small dinner parties and serve decent wine. She'd wear only her own creations and conversation would revolve around her shows at Fashion Week.

It'd be so much better than shuffling between her parents' dumps, getting wasted with Marjorie, and sleeping with losers.

"Okay," she'd said to the counselor, rubbing her temples.

"I can talk to Mr. Johnson," he said. "But he's a tough nut and you really need to pull your grades up in there to make this work."

She thought of the Theatre of the Absurd play and how she hadn't even tried. The night before it'd been due, the assignment had crossed her mind, but she was sitting at a picnic table outside a Mexican food cart drinking margaritas with Marjorie and thought, *Screw it. This is real life. This is fun. A cute boy across the parking lot keeps looking at me and there's no way I'm going to the boring library to do homework right now.*

At the time, she hadn't known there was a chance of graduating at the end of her junior year or what that would even mean, but now that a possible, happier future was beginning to take shape in her mind, she had more at stake than she'd suspected.

She forced herself to pay attention to the Cézanne slides her teacher was showing on the white screen at the front of the room. Fruit. Naked woman. Trees. Mountain. Men playing cards around a table. More fruit. So boring and expected. Impressionists were not her thing.

She much preferred the crazy boldness of Picasso. Not only did he have the talent to paint anything and paint it well, but he expanded on that, experimenting with the human form like no one else in history.

That was how she wanted her designs to be. Fresh, different, strong. She wanted to be the cubist of the fashion world. As she sat there in the darkened room among her quietly murmuring, shuffling classmates, she realized that she wanted it more than she wanted to party with Marjorie. More than she wanted to be liked by boys.

As she left class, Marjorie charged at her. "Two items of interest!" she bellowed. Because she could never say things at normal volume.

Trix's brain was still inside her ambitious haze. And she was hesitant to emerge into the real world of high school again. "What?" she said, and sighed.

"Number one: Do you want to join my band?"

"What band?"

"The band I'm starting. Machine Room."

"I don't play anything."

"None of us do! We'll learn."

Flattered, Trix almost said yes. But then she thought about the art institute and how she needed to focus on her schoolwork if she wanted to graduate early. "I can't," she said.

"What?" Marjorie cupped a hand around her ear. "I don't think I heard that right."

"I can't. I have too much … shit to do right now."

Marjorie was seriously put out. "Can you be more specific?"

"I need to get my grades back up. I have a chance at something and don't want to blow it."

Kids whizzed around them as if Trix and Marjorie were pinball bumpers. Marjorie yelled, "But you're so good at blowing it."

Trix treated Marjorie to one of her most condescending sneers and started to walk away.

"Wait, one more thing."

Trix turned on one heel and raised an eyebrow like a wicket.

"Ryan dumped your friend. He knocked up some other stupid bitch."

The air rushed from Trix's lungs and she had to remind herself to breathe so she'd have a voice. "He broke up with Emily."

"Yup, he's going to be a baby daddy."

She tried desperately not to look as shocked as she felt. She never would've pegged Ryan as someone who'd get a girl pregnant. And, the fact that he was and that he had ... could she still feel the same way about him? She liked squeaky-clean Ryan, impeccably respectable Ryan, too-good-for-her Ryan. If he was smarmy, he was just like all the guys she'd been with in her lifetime. "Huh, wow," she said, deadpan.

Marjorie started singing "Baby daddy, baby daddy," as she walked away from Trix, down the hall.

Trix felt sick in the very pit of her stomach but also astonished, because the ants had finally stilled.

57. LIFT OFF

THE THING EMILY loved best about flying was the jet zooming down the runway at two hundred miles an hour, trees and buildings whooshing by, then the nose lifting and wheels leaving the ground. The speed. The rush. It was better than any drink she'd ever tried. Almost as good as finding out a boy you liked liked you back.

But Emily wouldn't think about that.

She pressed her forehead against the cold window, wishing she could listen to her iPod, but knowing electronic devices weren't allowed yet. Below, the world had pulled away and now everything looked like the small cars and tracks and town sets she and Kristen had played with when they were little.

Bridges crisscrossed Seattle: the Ballard, the Aurora, the Fremont, the I-5, and then the floating bridges leading to the Eastside. The Puget Sound was gray and choppy and shrinking below her like a spreading stain in reverse. Then, through mottled clouds she could see mountains. One in particular: Mt. Rainier, still amazing to her even though she'd lived near it all her life. It rose thousands of feet higher than the rest of the Cascade Range and hulked, like a giant among children.

Finally, the pilot came on the sound system and announced it was okay to use electronics again. Emily fired up some MGMT, opened a book she had to read for Johnson's class, and tried to lose herself.

58. CHRISTMAS EVE

TRIX'S DAD HAD left town for Christmas. He'd gone to stay with a friend on an Indian reservation in Eastern Washington. And Trix wasn't invited. As little as she cared about the holiday, she couldn't just hang out alone at her dad's depressing duplex, so she took the bus back to the trailer on Aurora and let herself in. She thought maybe she and her mom could do their usual pancake house brunch in the morning, then catch a matinee. She hoped Rodney was busy doing something else.

She found Fiona sitting on the couch, a thin, clear tube running from a small tank on the floor into her mother's nostrils. "Oxygen," she said. "I've been getting tired so fast lately. It's the tank for me now."

On TV, a talk show blared.

Trix turned it down and said, "What? Forever?"

Rotating her palms up, her mom said, "Unless they find a cure."

Trix didn't think Fiona looked distressed enough for having just been hooked to a leash for life.

"Jesus, Ma." Trix took off her coat and set a flat, wrapped box—holding a shirt she'd designed and sewed in the home ec room at school—on the coffee table.

Her mother just nodded, eyes still on the TV screen. "It'll happen to you, too. If you keep smoking."

Trix couldn't even think about that right then. Old age seemed so incredibly far away, and her current life too stressful to stop smoking. Later, she thought. When I turn 18.

"I have other news," Fiona said, a small smile creeping across her face.

Trix was still distracted by the oxygen tank at her mother's feet. "What's that?"

"I'm marrying Rodney."

It was then that Trix noticed the skinny silver band on her mother's ring finger. "Merry Christmas to me!" Fiona said and laughed her old smoker's laugh.

"Please tell me this is a joke," Trix said. "You've known him for what? Two months."

Fiona waved away her daughter's concern. "Oh, when you're as old as me, it all happens quicker."

Trix stood and strode agitatedly toward the kitchen, looking for coffee. Even a half-full pot of cold coffee she could heat in the microwave. But there was none. She wanted a cigarette. That was out of the question, of course. She found a can of Diet Rite in the fridge and popped it open. It seemed entirely possible that she could hyperventilate. If her mom married Rodney, Trix knew she could never live here again. Not that she had a burning desire to, but she had no idea how long her dad would be willing to put up with her.

I've gotta get into the Art Institute, she thought. She could pay for housing with financial aid. That would mean another nine months before she could live on her own.

"Mom," she said. "Please tell me you're going to have a long engagement."

"We're thinking spring."

Christ!

"It'll just be small. At the courthouse. Pizza and beer after."

Trix didn't like this one bit. She paced. She wondered if he was coming over that night. "What about breakfast tomorrow? Are we doing the pancake thing?"

Fiona looked at Trix, then knocked the oxygen tank with her knuckles. "I'm not ready to go out with this thing on, yet, Trixie."

"A movie? I was thinking maybe the new Judd Apatow flick. A theater will be dark ... "

Her mother rapped the tank again.

Fine, then. Fiona was going to have fun being a bride hooked to that behemoth.

Trix went into her room and slammed the door. It was just as she'd left it. Bed unmade, dresser drawers half open, closet mostly cleared out. She sat on the mattress edge and drank her soda.

This felt nothing like Christmas Eve. Nothing at all. Her mom had at least made an effort when Trix was younger, with an artificial tree and stockings, but now it might as well be March 23rd. There was nothing in this trailer that would give away the date as December 24th.

"Don't worry," Fiona yelled from the other room. "You won't have to call him Daddy!" Her smoky cackle erupted again.

Counting her money might cheer her up, so Trix reached under her bed for the shoebox.

Something was wrong. The box was there, but as she pulled it out, it felt lighter than it should. In fact, it felt empty.

Frantic, she yanked off the top and stared at the four cardboard walls that surrounded nothing but air. Where was her sewing machine fund?

Barreling back out in the living area, Trix said, "Ma, I was saving money in this box. Where'd it go?"

Fiona's eyes barely flicked away from the TV.

"What do you mean saving money?"

"You know, putting it away for the future, for something I wanted to buy!" Trix yelled.

"How would I know?"

"Because you're always here and I haven't been much. Where's my money?"

Suddenly, Fiona looked at her daughter, but instead of empathetic disappointment on behalf of Trix, there was a moony gaze of admiration. "So that's where it came from."

"What Ma? That's where what came from?"

"Rod said he came across some money to buy my ring." Fiona held her hand out and ogled the cheap silver band.

Trix was on the verge of screaming and crying. "That was my money."

"Well, how was he supposed to know?"

"It was under my bed!"

"Maybe so, but I deserve nice things, too."

"I worked my butt off for that cash."

She couldn't believe this. Not only was her mom marrying Rodney the creep, but he'd stolen what was hers and now she was going to have to start saving all over again.

"You're young," Fiona said, turning her attention back to her show. "You'll earn more."

Trix threw the shoebox on the floor and charged out of the house, tears coursing down her face. She was sure her mascara was all over the place, but she didn't care. She stood on the fake-grass "patio" and shakily lit a cigarette.

"Don't you smoke that around here!" her mom called through the door.

Trix started to walk. She didn't know where she was going. She didn't care. Just somewhere else. Anywhere else.

As she strode down Aurora, her crappy cell phone trilled. It was Marjorie asking if she wanted to go to a bonfire at Golden Gardens.

She wavered for a moment, then texted back, "Ok." At least it was a destination.

59. LANDED

SOUTHEAST ARIZONA WAS hot. And dry. So hot and dry that Emily had to apply lip balm five times on the 90-mile trip along I-10 and Highway 80 from Tucson to Bisbee. This particular shuttle, her second shuttle of the day, was a rusted white van with ripped upholstery. The interior smelled like a decomposing rodent.

She was travel weary, but also excited and nervous and nauseated.

By now her dad knew all about her trip. Was he storming around the house calling Melissa names? Or hiding in his office, giving her and Kristen the silent treatment?

Emily was too scared to check her phone. It had been off all day. She worried that if she looked at it and saw she had voice mail, she'd listen. And if she listened, she'd hear her father ranting like a lunatic. And if she heard him ranting, her backbone would crumble to dust and she'd stay holed up in the youth hostel all three days.

So she kept her cell phone safely tucked in her backpack and stared through the grimy, tinted windows at stretches of spiny cacti, and coppery hills. Lots of Harleys and trucks towing silver Airstreams passed the "shuttle." A vulture circled the cloudless sky. Emily imagined she could see the van as the vulture could, a flat, white rectangle zooming toward Bisbee.

An older couple sat in the row behind Emily, the man giving a running commentary on the scenery. Every sentence was punctuated by, "Well, will you look at that!"

In front of her was a guy in his mid-twenties or so, who wore lime green glasses and voraciously read *The Corrections* by Jonathan Franzen, a book Ryan liked. Emily swallowed the now-familiar tartness that lingered in the back of her throat.

When the shuttle entered Bisbee, a small old-west looking town surrounded by orange, terraced hills and copper mines, Emily's mouth went dry again.

The van dropped her off in front of a RE/MAX real estate office. She tipped the driver three dollars and stood there watching him pull away, her backpack over her shoulders, a Google map in her hand.

The buildings were two or three stories high, bay windows pushing out over the narrow street, small signs hanging across doorways. She couldn't take in any other details. She was too distracted by her final destination: Marilyn Wozniak's house.

The air at the higher altitude was cool, almost misty. This disappointed Emily. She wanted the heat of Tucson. The break from drizzle and clouds. But then, she wasn't there for a vacation, was she? She'd come to Bisbee, Arizona for answers.

She checked her map. Marilyn lived three-quarters of a mile west, on a street called Harrison. Emily began to walk. She went until the buildings thinned and the sidewalks disappeared. She'd never been so nervous. How would her mother react? What if she hid and wouldn't open the door? Or yelled? Or cried? Or called the police? Or wasn't there at all?

Twice on her trek, Emily stopped and ambled in small circles along the side of the road. Could she really do this? She was terrified.

Each time, she took a deep breath and ventured on. She hadn't blown $350 she could've spent on new jeans just to loiter on the decaying pavement.

Emily slowed as she approached Marilyn's block. She gulped in deep breaths and crossed her arms over her chest. She checked the address two more times and licked her parched lips.

There was a car in the driveway. An old Volvo. The house was barely visible through a wooden fence tangled with ferocious vines. Emily peeked through a couple of slats. She saw an overgrown yard, a small iron table and chairs, a trellis leading up to a weathered front door.

Her mother lived there.

60. PEACE ON EARTH

WHEN TRIX GOT to Golden Gardens, it was dark and drizzly, but she could easily see the roaring bonfire on the beach. Around it were the silhouettes of kids holding beers.

Marjorie called, "Hey Bi-otch!" and offered Trix a cigarette. Gratefully, Trix took it. "Merry Christmas! That's all I got you."

Trix laughed and said, "It'll do." Screw Christmas anyway. It was just some stupid day for families with little kids. She took a long drag on the cigarette, was handed a PBR, and popped it open. Maybe this would become her new Christmas Eve tradition. Beach party. Could be a whole lot worse.

She thought about Emily, probably having a perfect family get-together, roasting marshmallows in the fireplace or some such B.S. For a moment, Trix felt immensely relieved by her freedom. She wasn't the type who'd do well with a full family and the associated rituals. She'd chafe, wanting to be out with her friends.

So, here she was. Celebrating on the beach with a bunch of other kids. And a few people who looked of age. Or older. Whatever. She was just glad she'd escaped her thieving mother.

Trix sat on an old log, the front of her scalded by the heat of the flames, the back of her cold. The orange glow from the fire flickered against everyone's faces. Someone had pulled their car up to the edge of the parking lot, opened their windows, and was blasting The Shins.

"It's not exactly Jingle Bells," Trix said. A guy to her left laughed.

"Thank God," He said.

She wondered who all these people were. Misfits. Transplants. Kids without real families. Isaac was there. And his friend Adam, too. She didn't recognize anyone else.

The guy next to her said, "So, what's your story? Why aren't you riding in a sleigh or sipping hot chocolate under the mistletoe?"

"Right."

She found out his name was Jamie when another guy called across the fire to him. "What about you?" she asked. "No twinkling lights on your Christmas tree?"

"I'm a Jehovah's Witness," he said.

"Aha."

"And you're all pagans." Jamie said and laughed. He was twenty-one and had moved to Seattle from Butte, Montana. He lived in the parking lot of Fred Meyer, sleeping in the back of his truck and peeing in the bushes at night. He said he took the occasional job as a day laborer, but mostly liked to hang out at the beach.

Loser, Trix thought. But as the night wore on and she consumed more beer, she started to admire him. Talk about freedom. Besides, he was hot, with caramel skin, black hair, and arm muscles that rippled when he tossed logs onto the fire.

Marjorie raised her brows at Trix and mouthed, "Sa-weet!"

"So you're going to art school?" Jamie asked, passing a bong her way.

Taking a hit, she said, "The sooner the better."

"That's cool. I like artsy girls."

She was in that perfect buzzed state, floaty and warm. She hadn't begun the descent that always came, when she felt dizzy and sick and exhausted. *Please let this last. It's my one Christmas wish.*

The Puget Sound was so dark that, without the lap of the tide coming in or the salty smell drifting up and down the beach, you'd never know it was there.

The year before, Trix and Fiona had gone to Emily's family's house for Christmas dinner and it had been dismal. Bob Lucas couldn't stop working, even on that one day, and he kept disappearing into his office. Melissa burbled around, overcompensating for everyone else's lack of enthusiasm. She played retro holiday songs and served vegan eggnog and wheatgrass cookies.

This, what she was doing now, was how Trix wanted to spend every Christmas.

The music played, a psychedelic, slow drumbeat with a crooning violin and deep male voice. In the brackish midnight air, Trix found herself dancing, her feet digging into the sand, warm on top but cold underneath. She went in circles around the fire, laughing with the others who'd joined her.

Someone threw a piece of driftwood into the flames and sparks flew, causing excited screams to erupt. Trix kept dancing. She would dance and party so hard that night, she wouldn't notice the crash when she fell.

61. WELCOME?

SLOWLY, EMILY OPENED the gate. It squealed and she almost bolted. She didn't know if she could walk right up to Marilyn's house and knock on the door.

Gingerly, she closed it behind her and continued on.

Her hands were shaking and she wanted to whimper, to run. Instead, she knocked.

A small dog barked. Someone told the dog to be quiet. Footsteps. The crack of the door loosening from its frame. A giant man's face, then body. He had scant gray hair, a thin beard. He was far taller than Emily. Winslow, she thought.

Clearing her throat, Emily asked, "Is Marilyn home?"

"Well, yes. But she's indisposed at the moment." He looked at Emily curiously, probably thinking she was some Greenpeace volunteer who'd whip out a clipboard at any moment and ask him to sign a petition.

"I, um, I'm not selling anything. I'm an old friend."

"What did you say your name was?"

"Emily."

The name didn't seem to ring a bell with him. This annoyed her, but she continued to stand there with the pleasantest look she could muster plastered across her face.

Winslow turned and behind the door shouted, "Marilyn! Someone named Emily is here to see you!"

Now she knew. Now Marilyn could choose not to come to the door at all.

But there was shuffling. The dog yipped again. Through a window, Emily spotted a small, potted palm, adorned with white lights and a few decorations.

Then there she was. Marilyn stood eye-to-eye with Emily, her brow furrowed, her coral lips parted in confusion. She pulled the lapels of her ivory blouse together, as if she were in a bathrobe. Her hair was long and frizzy, her face thin, just like in her picture. "You're Emily?"

"That's me." Already, Emily knew coming was a mistake. No one had been pining for her or thinking about her. She wasn't welcome.

What could she do though? She was there. "Merry Christmas!" she chirped and forced herself to smile.

"Why, I—"

"I know, I know. It's a shock. Your long-lost daughter shows up at your door on Christmas Eve. Uninvited. I just … I brought you something." She set her backpack on the step and dug through it. She pulled out a photo album she'd hastily put together the day before, swiping old pictures of her and Kristen from albums Melissa had constructed over the years.

"I don't have anything for you," Marilyn said brusquely.

"That's okay. You didn't even know I'd be here." Though in her heart of hearts, Emily had fantasized about her mother pulling her inside and showing her the gifts and trinkets she'd been collecting for her since she'd left so many years ago, she knew that wasn't realistic. She already understood her mother was an unsentimental sort.

Marilyn took the album, wrapped in spangly red and green paper, and acted like she didn't know what to do with it. Finally, she tucked it under one arm. "Well, I suppose … do you want to come in?"

"Sure!" Emily crowed. She wanted to weep.

Watching her mother's body move, a replica of what Emily would probably look like in the distant future, fascinated and saddened her. There she was, the woman who'd birthed Emily and raised her for the first four years, and yes, she was tall. But she wasn't especially graceful or inspiring.

Jazzy Christmas music played. Emily set her backpack down at the front door, took off her shoes on a woven straw mat, and followed Marilyn and Winslow inside.

The walls were stucco, painted a color Emily remembered from her crayon box: burnt sienna. A fire crackled in a rounded fireplace. Mugs half full of coffee sat on TV trays. The palm tree winked at her, mockingly. How could Marilyn Wozniak be having such a homey holiday with her new husband while her former family plodded along up north?

She pushed her anger down again. She didn't come here to fight with her mother.

Marilyn set her gift on the arm of a denim sofa. She asked, "Would you like some cocoa, or ... ?"

"Coffee'd be great."

"Really? Oh, yes. Winslow?"

He bustled off to the kitchen, having to duck, Emily noticed, through the doorframe.

"Have a seat," Marilyn said. She may as well have added, *Since you've barged in on my Christmas Eve.* She was as warm and welcoming as a tree trunk.

"Thanks." Emily perched on the edge of a plaid chair.

"You're a smidge taller than me," Marilyn said. "Taller than I expected."

"I'm taller than everyone expected."

"Ah well," she said. "There are worse things."

That may be the case, but Marilyn, stealing quick glances at Emily, seemed to regard her as an alien life form.

Winslow came back with the coffee. He never asked how Emily took it (with cream and sugar), so she just sipped it black.

Emily had a million questions. None of which seemed appropriate to ask.

"So, your father is doing well, I trust," Marilyn asked.

"Yeah, he's fine. He works a lot."

Marilyn's mouth twisted. "He always did. Too afraid of not having a hundred thousand dollars in the bank at all times."

Emily's father and Marilyn certainly seemed like the ultimate mismatch: conservative, money-obsessed Bob Lucas and this eccentric woman.

"Can I ask you a question?" Emily said.

"I'm assuming that's why you're here."

"How did you and my dad meet?" As she asked, she wondered why she hadn't had this conversation with her father. Ever. What was wrong with them that they hadn't even discussed such a simple but important fragment of the past?

Her eyes darted toward Winslow, then settled on the snapping fire. "At a bar."

Somehow, this didn't surprise Emily. She couldn't imagine another scenario where Marilyn and her dad would've been in the same room.

"You may as well know," Marilyn said. "Your sister was the product of what was supposed to be a one-night stand."

Winslow retrieved a fire poker, his face a placid lake. He must already know this story.

"Really?" Emily's face burned. The idea of her father and mother drunk and groping was not at all appealing. "But you had me, too."

Peripherally, she saw Winslow jabbing at the fire, adding a log.

"For a while I thought I could do the family thing. I tried. I did. But it wasn't right for me."

Then Emily did what she swore to herself she wouldn't. She said, her voice low with fury, "What about what was right for your daughters?"

Marilyn yanked a tissue out of her sleeve and dabbed the inner corners of her eyes. This heartened Emily the tiniest bit. Remorse. "I thought about that. Of course, I did. But I'm just not meant to be a mother." She didn't come right out and say *I'm selfish*, but that was what Emily took away from Marilyn's confession. It was what she'd always known about her mother.

Emily's coffee had cooled, but for something to do, she drank it anyway. "He remarried," she said, hoping to hurt Marilyn the same way Marilyn had hurt Emily and Kristen. "To a great person. Melissa. She's just … amazing." She realized she meant it. Melissa had overcome so much. She'd come through her miscarriage. She lived with Emily's dad and still managed to love him. She gave more attention and time to Emily and Kristen than most actual mothers would. She was ten times the person Marilyn Wozniak was.

"I'm sure he's very happy," Marilyn said.

Emily would not tell her that *happy* and her dad were mutually exclusive. So she just muttered, "Yep."

There was a long, awkward silence. Finally, Winslow turned from the fire he was compulsively prodding and said, "So what brings you this way, Emily?"

"Oh," she said. "You know. I've always wanted to meet Marilyn, here. And I had a break from school, so I figured this was as good a time as any. I'm sorry I didn't tell you I was coming. I was just … afraid you'd say no if I asked."

He nodded, his gray mustache scrunching up under his nose.

"Well, do you have anywhere else to go? Would you like to stay for dinner?"

Truthfully, no, she didn't want to stay for dinner. She wanted to beam herself back to her bedroom where she could ruminate over this whole thing. But meeting Marilyn and getting to know her were the reasons she'd come to Bisbee at all. "Um, sure. That's really nice of you. I'm staying at a hostel in town, but a meal would be great," she added, so they'd know she wasn't hoping for a bed later. She purposely didn't look in Marilyn's direction. She couldn't handle seeing an expression that held even a hint of reluctance.

"All righty. We're having duck confit with pear salad and rustic rosemary dinner rolls. Think you can choke that down?"

So, Winslow was a foodie. She'd never eaten duck before, but all she'd consumed that day was a snack pack of almonds, a few Oreos, and a bag of chips. "Yeah, no problem."

Oddly, her mind lurched to Trix. What was she doing on Christmas Eve with darkness falling? Were she and her mom at their annual movie, planning a pancake house brunch for the next morning? Or was Trix hanging out with Marjorie, trying to pretend Christmas didn't exist?

Emily shook her head. She didn't want to think about Trix then. She had enough going on.

Winslow shuffled to the kitchen and there was much clanging of pots and pans.

Marilyn, instead of using the time to chat with Emily one-on-one, said, "I'll go see if he needs help."

Emily called after her, "Is there anything I can do?"

"No! No, that's all right. You just … relax."

Emily leaned her head back against the rough stucco wall and let out a long breath. This was horrible. Worse, she decided, than being turned away at the door.

62. JOY TO THE WORLD

"MY TRUCK'S PARKED just over there in the lot," Jamie said.

The music had quieted. The fire only smoldered. Almost everyone had left. Trix, Jamie, Marjorie, Isaac and a few others sat on cold driftwood, smoking. Trix shivered and tried to figure out how to get back to her dad's. It was late and the buses were operating on a holiday schedule. It'd be hours before one would come by.

Suddenly, she badly wanted to see her cat, to bury her face in his fur and sleep.

Jamie asked, "Need a ride somewhere?"

She stood, depressed that her perfect buzz was on the downslide, and tugged her jacket around her waist. "Let's go." She gave Marjorie the peace sign and strode across the asphalt, which was lit with yellow streetlights. She only stumbled once or twice.

"Careful, sister," Jamie said, catching and righting her.

In the distance, sailboat lines clanked on masts and water sloshed against docks.

Jamie's truck was an old Ford with a cap on the back. She expected him to unlock the cab doors, but instead he popped open the tailgate to reveal a foam mattress and several paper grocery bags full of clothes, CDs, and other miscellaneous stuff.

"This is my setup," he said.

"Wow," she said, not sure if she was sarcastic or sincere.

"You wanna test it out?"

"I'm not stupid." She knew what he would try if she crawled in there and lay down.

"I never said you were."

On the other hand, the mattress looked soft and she was weary. "Okay," she agreed and climbed in. She reclined and, in a moment, the truck creaked and the tailgate slammed shut. Jamie was next to her, already breathing heavily. Jeez. She really didn't need this tonight of all nights. "So, I'm assuming you won't be giving me a ride in the near future."

"You'll get your ride. Just relax for now. You were doing a lot of dancing."

She sighed loudly. She went to sit up, and then realized she was still quite drunk. Dizzily, she put her head back onto the mattress.

Jamie said, "I love how you move."

"You do?"

"Yeah. I couldn't take my eyes off you."

She had a feeling she'd heard this before, yet she ate it up. He was making her feel special and less lonely. He was giving her what she thought she wanted.

"Tell me about art school," he said, as he nibbled at her neck. It felt good. His lips were soft and warm, his body taut next to her. It was too dark to see him, but she remembered his black hair and burnished skin. She reached up and felt his ropey arms.

As they kissed, his hands went up her shirt.

63. UNWANTED

TO TAKE HER mind off the horribleness of being somewhere she was not wanted, Emily pulled out her phone and checked her messages. There were three from her father, which she skipped. Her heart leapt when she saw one from Ryan. As fast as her fingers would work, she connected to voice mail.

"Hey, Bean. I mean, Emily. I just wanted to say Merry Christmas. I, uh, I can't believe … um, scratch that. I hope you're having a good day, that's all. I'm skiing with my folks. So, you know, Merry Christmas."

She sucked in her cheeks and frantically jiggled one knee over the worn plaid chair in Bisbee, Arizona. *Don't cry don't cry don't cry.*

After a few minutes, she inhaled and dialed Melissa's cell.

Melissa picked up on the second ring.

"I'm here," Emily said quietly.

"Where's here? The airport? Your hostel? Your mother's?"

"Yeah, Marilyn's."

"Wow," Melissa said. "Wow. So, is it okay?"

"Mostly, I guess." Emily couldn't admit, right then, that traveling to see a woman who'd already proven to be an apathetic, selfish, old burr oak was not the most logical or rewarding thing to do on Christmas Eve.

"Mostly," Melissa echoed.

"Well, I mean, things never turn out how you fantasize they will." Emily picked at a loose piece of rubber on her sneaker. "How's dad taking it?"

"Oh, not well. Didn't you get his messages?"

"I haven't listened to them."

"We knew how he'd react, right? So, he's living up to our expectations. He'll get over it."

"Melissa?" Emily said. "Thank you. I mean, like, thank you so much for going to bat for me and helping me do this. However things go with Marilyn, I needed to come here and you knew that, and I couldn't have done it without you." She stopped before her voice caught. Her emotions were all over the place.

"I know, honey. I know."

Emily wondered if she loved Melissa. She thought she might. She knew she could. Melissa, young, pretty Melissa, had chosen to parent her and Kristen. And, yeah, maybe they were fulfilling some mommy fantasy for Melissa, but who cared? It was working.

"Thank you," Emily said again.

"Okay, you need to stop thanking me now or I'm going to bawl."

"Me too." Emily laughed and wiped at a hot tear that had spilled down her cheek.

"So, are you staying there?"

"Just for dinner. Duck. I'm sleeping at the hostel. They're being polite, letting me eat with them. But they don't want me here."

"They don't know you well enough then. They'll learn how delightful you are."

"Oh, stop. All right, I guess I should go. Merry merry," Emily said. "Tell Dad and Kristen that, too."

"I will. Call me tonight from the hostel, okay? Or better yet, call your dad's cell. I think it'll help."

Ugh. The last thing she wanted to do was talk to her seething father. But she knew Melissa was right. "I guess," she said.

"Seriously, Em. Promise you'll call your dad tonight. He needs to hear from you. It'll make it easier on all of us."

"All right. I promise."

"Good. Thank you."

And they signed off.

Emily texted Thomas then. *@ Marilyn's. Den of hostility.*

Thomas texted back right away. *Sorry darlin. Hugs. Xoxo.*

Emily was tense, wound up more tightly than a rubber band ball.

To blow off steam, she quietly pulled her camera out of her backpack, dialed down the aperture to let in more light, and began to snap photos of the living room.

She squatted in front of a window and took a photo of the cactus on the sill. She shot the Christmas palm and the dog bed with a chewed up plastic toy next to it. Emily could totally imagine the photos in sepia, forming a sort of bleak collage of her trip to Bisbee.

From the kitchen wafted the smells of meat and spices. Emily's stomach growled, yet she didn't want to eat the food there. McDonald's would be preferable to feeling indebted.

When they sat down to dinner, she closed her eyes and held her hands in her lap while Winslow said a prayer. They had poured her, she noticed, a glass of red wine. She didn't really like wine, but she took a courteous sip.

"Just a little '02 Cab Franc," Winslow explained.

The rich wine that Winslow described as "oaky" coursed down her throat, warming her stomach and making her face flush. It was good. Delicious, in fact. She took another sip.

"There's a big difference between this and the swill you kids probably guzzle," he said.

"Oh, well, I don't normally drink wine. Or drink much at all. But this is really great."

Marilyn ate silently, her eyes cast down on her meal. Could she be remembering Christmases past? Christmases with Emily and Kristen?

The dog paced around and around the table.

Emily ate, trying to ignore her mother's iciness. She still couldn't get used to the fact that the woman who'd given birth to her was just across the table.

She finished her glass of wine and Winslow refilled it. Twice. By the end of dinner, Emily was seriously buzzed.

Marilyn had asked her exactly two questions during the meal. 1. Did she enjoy school? And 2. What was her favorite subject? Inquiries adults made to be polite, when they had no interest in knowing the real You.

Emily had answered accordingly. 1. It was okay. And 2. English.

The conversation was horribly stilted. Worse, even, than Emily could have imagined.

After a dessert of pumpkin tart, Emily rubbed her uncomfortably full stomach, deciding she'd wait a little while before calling her dad. She knew she was too tipsy right then to contact him. He'd pick up on it and that would set him off like a firecracker.

Winslow guided Marilyn and Emily to the living room where he brought out a bottle of Port and proceeded to fill miniature glasses with the liquid that looked as thick and dark as blood.

When Emily first tasted it, she coughed. It was sickeningly sweet. But Winslow closed his eyes appreciatively while Marilyn sipped and stared into space. The jazzy Christmas music still played.

"So, do you remember spending any holidays with us?" Emily asked, emboldened by the wine and port.

Marilyn looked stricken. She glanced at Winslow, who was serenely sipping. Then, in almost a whisper, she hissed, "Of course I do."

"But you never miss them? Miss us?"

"I told you," Marilyn said. "I wasn't cut out to be a mother."

"Too bad you didn't figure that out before becoming one, huh? You could've saved us all a lot of grief."

Marilyn's mouth opened as if she were about to speak, then closed. Her lips thinned and she gazed into the lit tree.

"Let's try to get along, ladies," Winslow intercepted. Extravagantly, he added, "It's Christmas!"

Fury sizzled across Emily's skin like a sunburn, but she bit her lips hard to keep from saying another mean thing.

64. GIVING IT UP

"IT'LL FEEL GOOD," Jamie said. "I promise."

The back of the truck was cold, the mattress so thin Trix could feel frigid metal when she shifted her weight. A car rumbled by.

"Duh," Trix said. He'd been peeling her shirt up toward her shoulders when she uncharacteristically stopped him. "Of course it'll feel good. That's what you all say."

"Because it's true." His voice was flinty, almost angry.

"Can't we just lie here and talk?" She sounded simpering and this disgusted her. Still, to just connect with him, with someone, verbally was what she wanted right then.

"Just snuggle?" he scoffed.

"Yeah, kinda. It's Christmas," she said. And she realized, as it came out of her mouth, that she really did care about it, that she missed her pancake dinners and movies with her mom.

Jamie began kissing her again, more insistently this time. He rose up slightly so he arched over her, his hands pinning her wrists to the mattress.

Trix felt herself stirring, her body responding to his. She could do this. It would be nice to lose herself for a while.

In her head, a voice spoke. The voice was a prism: part Emily, part her guidance counselor, part her dad, and part Trix herself: *Don't give in. It's not what you want. Not really.*

How do you know?

Because you'll never love yourself until you stop giving it up to any boy who wants your body.

Shut up.

Please?

Shut up.

Jamie pressed his pelvis into hers and started grinding.

Wanting her body wasn't the same as wanting her, she knew that. So why did she pretend it was?

"Take off your jeans," Jamie murmured.

65. NOT THE MOTHER SHE WOULD HAVE CHOSEN

EMILY COULD'VE KEPT it together if Winslow hadn't said, "You should be nice to your mother. She gave birth to you, after all. She gave you life."

Emily started to cry. Why had she thought a surprise visit to Marilyn would be a good idea? She'd rather have kept the fantasy that her mother was a shiny fashion model retired to the south of France or even a strung out drug addict in the city.

Tears coursing down her cheeks, Emily looked at Marilyn, really looked at her frizzy, long hair, gaunt face, the silver and turquoise earrings, the lack of concern in her eyes. She knew her visit had been a mistake. Or, if you took it another way, a wake-up call. Maybe that was good?

She stood, swaying, and said, "I'll just get my bag and go. I'll leave you alone. Thank you for dinner. Thank you for ... my life. I'm sorry I bothered you."

Neither Winslow nor Marilyn protested. They watched her over their glasses of port, the stupid, jazzy Christmas music still playing.

"Shall we call you a cab?" Winslow asked.

"I can walk," Emily grabbed her backpack and camera bag, fumbled with the doorknob, and burst out of the little, stucco house.

She couldn't help herself as she wobbled away—she looked back. She looked back hoping for a glimpse of her mother in the window, her hand to the glass, her eyes full. But all she saw was the palm plant dotted with white lights.

The night was cool and very dark. She wished she'd thought to pack a flashlight. Luckily, she had a decent sense of direction and, even drunkish, thought she could find her way to the hostel.

66. ESCAPE

"C'MON," JAMIE PRODDED, his fingers working Trix's jeans button.

Then, without thinking, without a single conscious thought directing her, Trix slapped his hand away.

She sat and tugged down the hem of her shirt. She crawled toward the closed tailgate and started banging at it.

"Hey! What the hell?"

"Let me out!"

"What? Why? Jesus!"

She kicked until the door of the cap popped open. She climbed over the cold metal tailgate and started to run.

"Seriously?" he bellowed. "Dicktease!"

She didn't care what he said. She didn't care. She ran on her high-heeled boots through the mist, the sailboats still sloshing and clanking. She had no idea how she'd get to her mom's or her dad's or wherever she was supposed to call home.

The wind felt good on her face. Her breath was hot and cold in her lungs. She wanted to laugh and suddenly she did, huge peals ripping through her. Her exhalations and low cackling filled the night.

She'd done it. She'd gotten away without giving in. And, though she didn't know how she'd get back to her dad's duplex other than on her own two feet, she felt free. Different from the pseudofreedom she'd claimed earlier. Free like she could make her own decisions about her body for once, like she wasn't shackled to her slutty identity.

Trix knew what it felt like now to turn a boy down. She'd do it again. And again after that until she found someone smart and kind who cared about her as much as she cared about him.

That night she walked three-and-a-half miles in her high heels and slept at her dad's with just David the cat for company. In the morning, Christmas morning, she made herself a pot of coffee from good beans she'd been saving and scrambled two eggs. She didn't have any presents to open and, though that was admittedly a little painful, she felt better than she had in a long time. She tried to consider her new freedom a gift in itself. Waking that day and feeling not exactly pure, but clean and hopeful, was a great thing.

She sat down with her sketchbook and, while David twirled around her legs at the rickety table, which was really a card table with an old sheet tossed over it, drew an angular model wearing a short shirt and long, flowy jacket with bell sleeves. Working her way down to a pair of stacked heel boots, she realized the apartment was dead quiet and got up to turn on the radio.

Jingle Bells quavered through the speakers. Trix went to change the station, then thought, *Oh, why not?* She could handle a few Christmas carols.

As she turned to go back to the table, she saw something tucked against the second-hand entertainment center that hadn't been there before. It was a white plastic bag taped closed. On top sat a crushed blue bow.

She went over to it, looking for clues as to what was inside. Finally, she just decided to open it.

Trix peeled the bag away and gasped.

It was a sewing machine. Not the used model she'd had her eye on, but one that looked brand new with 60 stitch functions and three different presser feet. She scrabbled at the box, yanking it open, removing the protective Styrofoam and gazing at the gleaming plastic machine.

Just then, her crappy cell phone rang.

She didn't recognize the number, but answered anyway. The first thing she heard was the rush of traffic. Or a river.

"Merry Christmas, babe!" her dad said.

"Hey, Dad, you too." Trix could hear the smile in her voice. "Where are you?"

"At a pay phone in Colville. What about you?"

"At home." And she realized that, even though she had no bedroom of her own at her dad's duplex, this was her home for now, at least until she graduated. "So, I just found a bag with a sewing machine inside."

Her dad laughed, a hearty chuckle she didn't hear from him often. "That's why I'm calling. I didn't have time to write out a gift tag or what have you."

"Thank you so much, Dad. It's the nicest thing—" Her voice caught on the words. She cleared her throat. "It's the nicest thing I've ever gotten."

"Maybe you can use it when you get into that fancy art school."

"I will. Before that. I'm going to set it up right now."

And she did. She spent Christmas day poring over the owner's manual and threading bobbins and mending some of her dad's torn flannel shirts. Trix was the most content she could remember having been in a long, long time.

Like the solid tracks she stitched across whatever fabric she could find in her dad's duplex, it finally seemed imaginable that her life might move forward in even rows stretching on and on as far as the eye could see.

67. WHERE AM I?

EMILY WOKE IN the hard hostel bed, a scratchy blanket around her waist. She heard a toilet flush. It took a minute for it all to come back. The night before. Her mother who couldn't have cared less that Emily had come. The sadness.

And then, because she couldn't not, she thought about Ryan and wondered what he'd started to say in his voice mail? He couldn't believe what? That they weren't together anymore? That he was going to be a father?

Then she remembered, it was Christmas morning.

She squeezed her eyes closed, wishing she were home, wishing she and Ryan were still together and would be seeing each other later that day, wishing she could at least call Trix and relay the ridiculous, painful details of the night before.

Emily realized she'd forgotten to call her dad and wondered how furious he was. Damn! Poor Melissa and Kristen. She'd promised.

Gray light filtered into the small room. She got dressed and took her turn in the small bathroom. Her stomach churned. She remembered the photo album she'd given Marilyn and how she'd glanced back on her way out and saw it sitting, still wrapped, on a low pine end table.

She went to the hostel's front desk and canceled her reservation for the remaining two nights. She called the airport shuttle service from her cell phone. Her plan was to go to Tucson and hang around the gates until she could fly back to Seattle on standby.

A couple hours later, after getting coffee and a scone from a café, she was loading into the ratty van again and driving through Bisbee. The hills surrounding the town made it feel tucked in and cozy. But also stifled. Isolated.

All she could think about was home. She wanted to put some distance between herself and this place where Marilyn Wozniak lived, distance between the girl Emily had been and the person she was becoming. She wasn't sure who that was yet, but knew that after the past three months she was a lot closer to finding out.

Postscript

EMILY WORE HER new jeans, which she'd finally ordered online, a cute pair of black ankle boots she'd found at Target, and a chocolate brown cardigan that had always served her well. She felt strangely, eerily calm.

The day was unusually warm and sunny for mid-March. Emily hopped off her bike and crouched to lock it, her heart pounding. In less than an hour she'd be on stage in front of the whole school.

To distract herself, she thought about sleeping over at Kennedy's that coming night. She'd done it twice before and both times they'd stayed up until two a.m. streaming episodes of Glee and Gossip Girl and talking. She was beyond surprised at how well she and Kennedy got along. There was none of the underlying antagonism she'd always felt with Trix or the squirmy fear that if she did well at something, her friend would feel insecure.

Emily still couldn't stomach the other two Farkettes and, thankfully, Kennedy seemed to have pulled apart from them like a small planet breaking free of its wobbly orbit.

Slinging her camera bag and backpack over her shoulder, Emily moved toward the hulking brick building and quickly realized she'd stepped in dog crap. She weaved toward a grassy patch to wipe her shoe clean.

"Hey, Bean," a male voice said from the other side of a massive oak. Ryan emerged, looking a little haggard and harder lived than he had earlier in the year. A week or two before, Jessie'd given birth to a baby girl and given it up for adoption. While no paternity tests had been done, the girl had apparently been born with a shock of curly brown hair and wide-set eyes that looked a lot like Ryan's.

"Hi," Emily said. She still couldn't help the smile that hijacked her face and the lift she felt when she saw him.

"I was waiting for you."

"So I see. I just, uh, had an unfortunate mishap."

Ryan laughed, then crouched and began loosening her shoe. While she stood like a flamingo, he scrubbed the sole with a dry leaf.

"How chivalrous," she teased.

"Anything for you," he looked up at her as he worked.

Emily and Ryan were tentatively resuming their friendship. They weren't officially dating. Ryan was too scarred for anything right then. Still, she liked his texts, his waves in the hallway, and the occasional times he waited and walked into school with her.

"Jeez, this is rank," he said.

"Sorry."

"Not your fault. It's the negligent dog owner's fault."

"Maybe it was some feral pug."

Ryan laughed again.

Emily had, as the pediatric endocrinologist predicted, continued to grow. Ryan, surprisingly, had grown some, too.

She still had him by several centimeters, but she could live with that.

In the fall, Kristen was going off to Wazoo, otherwise known as Washington State University, in Pullman. Emily would miss her. But she also suspected her perfect sister's absence might open up a space in her to grow, not physically, but emotionally. She knew she still had some flourishing to do and Kristen's being gone may help that along.

Emily's dad was still, well, Emily's dad. She wished she could say he'd mellowed, made work a lesser priority, but she couldn't. Since Emily met her mom, though, her sympathy for and acceptance of her dad had deepened some. His anger, his overworking, sprouted from fear. Fear that he'd lose what he held dear again; fear that he'd have to live in poverty like he had as a kid.

Those realizations didn't make him any easier to live with, they just helped her understand.

Still, Melissa managed to live with Bob Lucas quite happily. She was still drinking green smoothies and sitting on her yoga ball while analyzing data for local businesses. She often forwarded Emily sales ads for stores she knew carried long jeans.

And, instead of being embarrassed and snotty about it, Emily just replied, "Thanks!" and checked out the deals.

"Are you nervous?" Ryan asked.

"Yeah."

Like some old-time shoe salesman, Ryan held out Emily's ankle boot so she could slip her foot into it.

"Thanks," she said, feeling a little like a low-rent Cinderella.

For once, the school hallways were subdued and clean. A weak sun tried to project blocks of yellow onto the tile floor, but only cast silvery, early spring light.

It would be a while before the audience tromped up to the auditorium, filling the school with smells of cologne and cold air and grilled onions whisked in on the winter coats everyone still wore.

"You're early," she said.

Ryan grinned. "I wanted a good seat."

Once they reached Johnson's room, which was next to the auditorium, Ryan reached up and touched her cheek. "Break a leg."

The brush of his hand after so many months made her tingle. "Thank you."

"I'll be watching."

After they parted, time acted as if it were being blown and sucked and stopped up in a tunnel. It dragged interminably. It raced. Emily's hands flew over the keyboard as she sat in one of the student desks and completed last minute edits on her project.

And suddenly there was silence and the inhalation of hundreds of people. Johnson's voice blared through the sound system as he welcomed the audience to the first ever Spring Spectacle.

Backstage, Emily got to work hooking her laptop to the projector. She looped a headset over her ear and asked the kid working sound if he had the right tracks. He confirmed he did. She took deep breaths to calm her nerves.

She silently questioned her sanity. She reminded herself that she needed to do this, to prove herself, to show mean kids that everyone was unique and not to be made fun of.

Emily sat in the wings, through a group of seniors acting out a scene from Twilight, a boy Emily didn't recognize sitting on stool by himself playing an acoustic version of a Coldplay song, and Marjorie's "band" wearing hot pink boas and hooting like the siamangs Emily remembered from her trips to the Woodland Park Zoo.

Finally, the stage manager, a senior girl whose paintings were always displayed in school art shows, came up and asked Emily if she was ready. "You're on next," she said.

"Yup. I'm good," Emily said. Though she was anything but good. Her stomach writhed like an animal in pain and her hands shook. She knew Ryan was out there. The Farkettes. Trix might be somewhere in the building. Even Melissa and Kristen had come. She had to learn to be okay with being on stage though, with being a standout. It was her lot and she needed to own it.

Emily inhaled deeply, cloaked in the quiet shadows of backstage, when a movement from the side caught her eye. She looked up and saw Thomas, a shaft of light coming in through the door behind him. He held a paper-wrapped bouquet of calla lilies.

Emily skirted over and threw her arms around his skinny shoulders.

He whispered, "You can have these if you knock 'em dead."

"What if I don't?"

"You will."

"Thank you for coming," she said, breathless. "Truly."

Grinning, he said, "Afterward, you have to point out everyone to me. I need faces with names, girl."

She waved him away and skittered back into the wing where she stood stiffly.

Finally, she heard her name over the sound system and began the slow, surreal walk, pushing the cart with her computer and projector to the side of the stage. The auditorium was so quiet she could hear her shoes squeak.

A white screen descended from the ceiling behind her. Her music, a mashup of her favorite electronica and house tunes, thumped. The spotlight, hot and yellow, illuminated her. At the microphone, she cleared her throat and said, "Present Tense."

Then she proceeded to recite a poem she'd written in the days right after Ryan broke up with her:

"You may think I'm strong (I can be)

You may think I don't feel (I do)

You may think this is all a big game (it's not)

People say, 'It will get better when you're older'

People say, 'High school is not real life'

But to us

This all seems

Bitingly, excruciatingly, horridly, amazingly, thrillingly

Real."

She sat on a tall stool and tapped her keyboard. The spotlight faded. The beats throbbed and the first photo appeared onscreen. It was a black and white shot of Trix at Greenlake. The day after she'd had the one-night stand at Jason Bleak's party. She wore her fake-fur coat and over-the-knee suede boots. She looked to the left and her face was etched with profound sadness. Emily prayed Trix would like it. She thought Trix looked beautiful.

The image faded and in its place appeared an abandoned beer bottle on a bus stop bench. Then a line up of kids along the second floor hall, some in focus, some blurred, some studying, some caught in animated conversation.

Then Ryan, smiling enormously, his eyes squinting with joy, his teeth gleaming. A shot of Brenna Toast, an overweight freshman, looking soft and pensive appeared. The photos kept coming. There were seventy-six in all. Kids. Places they all went. Some, like a photo of a Fatty's burger and fries, were mildly humorous, but most, she hoped, would inspire thought and compassion.

Emily heard a few gasps, a few swells of laughter, and, as the last photo faded and the stage lights rose, thundering applause.

She couldn't help it, she grinned. She smiled until her cheeks ached, then gave a little wave and pushed her cart off stage. Johnson and a few kids were standing there, offering fist bumps and high fives, telling her it had been "awesome" and "rad" and "sick." She decided right then she wasn't going to adopt an *aw shucks* attitude. She'd worked hard on her presentation. "Thanks!" she bubbled.

The halls were bright compared to the auditorium. When she got to her backpack, she had three texts. Kristen: Good wrk, sis! Ryan: Blwn Awy. Thomas, who texted in full words and sentences: I'm going to take you out for a magnum of champagne. Epic, girl. Epic!

Emily couldn't remember the last time she'd felt so creatively satisfied. So vindicated. And she didn't know how long the feeling would last, so she was going to enjoy it.

Melissa showed up then and hugged Emily. When she pulled back, Melissa's eyes brimmed. She nodded and looked away. She whispered, "I took video of that for your dad."

Emily nodded. She couldn't speak or she'd start to cry.

TRIX SAT IN the dark auditorium. She'd never seen the photo Emily had taken of her and shown the entire school. Staring up at it on the huge screen, the theater full of hundreds of hushed kids and parents, she'd felt an avalanche of emotion: shock, respect for Emily and her talent to capture moments, trauma at the torment on her own face, serious annoyance.

Now a freshman was doing an Irish dance that Trix didn't know if she could sit through. She needed to splash her face with cool water, maybe smoke, though she was trying to quit. She whispered to Irony (a real name for a real girl whom Trix had been hanging out with lately), "I need a break."

Irony nodded. "You okay?"

"Yeah."

"Want me to come with you?"

"Nah," Trix said, and crept up the aisle, trying not to look at the faces she passed.

She blinked in the light of the hallway and shot to the bathroom. It was blissfully empty. She turned on a faucet, as cold as it would go, and cupped her hands under the running water. Trix could see her reflection; her lined eyes staring back at her, and decided not to ruin her makeup. Opening her fingers, she let the water run through them, turned off the tap, and stood there, wondering where to go next.

That was when she heard the toilet flush and saw, in the mirror, Emily emerge from a stall.

"Hey," Trix said, stiffening. She grabbed a rough paper towel, drying her hands and throwing it in the garbage.

"Hey," Emily said, her voice slow and gentle, as if she were talking to a wild animal she was trying not to scare away. "What'd you think?

"Of?" She still had a wall up when it came to Emily.

"The photo of you. From Green Lake."

"I don't even remember you taking it."

"Oh, well. You were pretty … distraught." Trix remembered well the days when Emily was her go-to if she was unglued. Luckily, the ungluing happened less now. "So," Emily said. "How are things?"

Trix looked at her ex-friend. Only, instead of feeling torn up inside, a sort of dull, nostalgic placidity fell over her. They'd had a lot of good times. And, though they both knew their friendship was basically over, it didn't have to be horrendously awkward when they ran into each other. They could make eye contact and say Hey. Right? They could be adults about this. She just hoped Emily wouldn't say she missed her, or try to get her to talk about the downward spiral she'd been coasting on until a few months ago.

"Things are great," Trix said and shrugged. She was mostly telling the truth. She'd shaken Marjorie and her druggie friends loose in a knock-down-drag-out the day after Christmas during which they screamed at each other in a Safeway parking lot.

Trix's mom had broken up with Rodney the Octopus guy after realizing he was stealing from her, too.

There were no boys for Trix. After Jamie at the beach, she'd understood that she needed to pull her act together before she could go out with anyone. So, to reduce temptation, she wasn't drinking, either. Which, considering that she was underage, was probably for the best.

"I noticed you've been in class more," Emily said warily.

"Yeah," Trix crossed her arms over her chest. "School's good. I mean, it's school, so how good can it be? But, it's better." She'd gotten her grades back up and was on track to graduate at the end of her junior year. She was going to apply to the Art Institute, and Irony's friends, some who were already professional graphic designers and seamstresses and painters who'd gone there, said Trix would definitely make it.

Emily said, "I'm glad."

"And you're still taking photos I see."

"My first love," Emily said and winced. She cleared her throat.

Clearly, they wouldn't touch the topic of Ryan.

Trix poked at her eyeliner in the mirror, then moved toward the door. "Okay, well, see you."

"Around. Yeah."

Trix was preternaturally calm as she found her way back to her seat, feeling oddly cleansed by her face to face with Emily and brimming with a sense of possibility. She imagined a bird—a sparrow or pigeon that had somehow swooped in through the front doors and flew around the auditorium's rafters.

Below the bird, notes were passed, insults were whispered, kisses were exchanged, feelings were hurt, friendships dissolved while others solidified.

And from up there, no one looked so different from anyone else, they were all just one big, undulating mass of people in various states of learning that they were okay.

Acknowledgments: I'd like to thank Kristy Alley for being such an astute and helpful reader, Tricia Scott for her discerning critique of Spectacle's *cover, Betsy Hudson for her keen eye and mad copyediting skills, Sarah Piazza for catching several of my ridiculous errors, my husband and kids for their patience while I wrote and revised and wrote and revised, Alice Peck for her encouragement, and the literary agents whose rejections led me to pursue my exciting e-publishing path.*

www.ingramcontent.com/pod-product-compliance
Lightning Source LLC
Chambersburg PA
CBHW060801120626
46557CB00001B/54